DEATH NOTE
ANOTHER NOTE
THE LOS ANGELES BB MURDER CASES

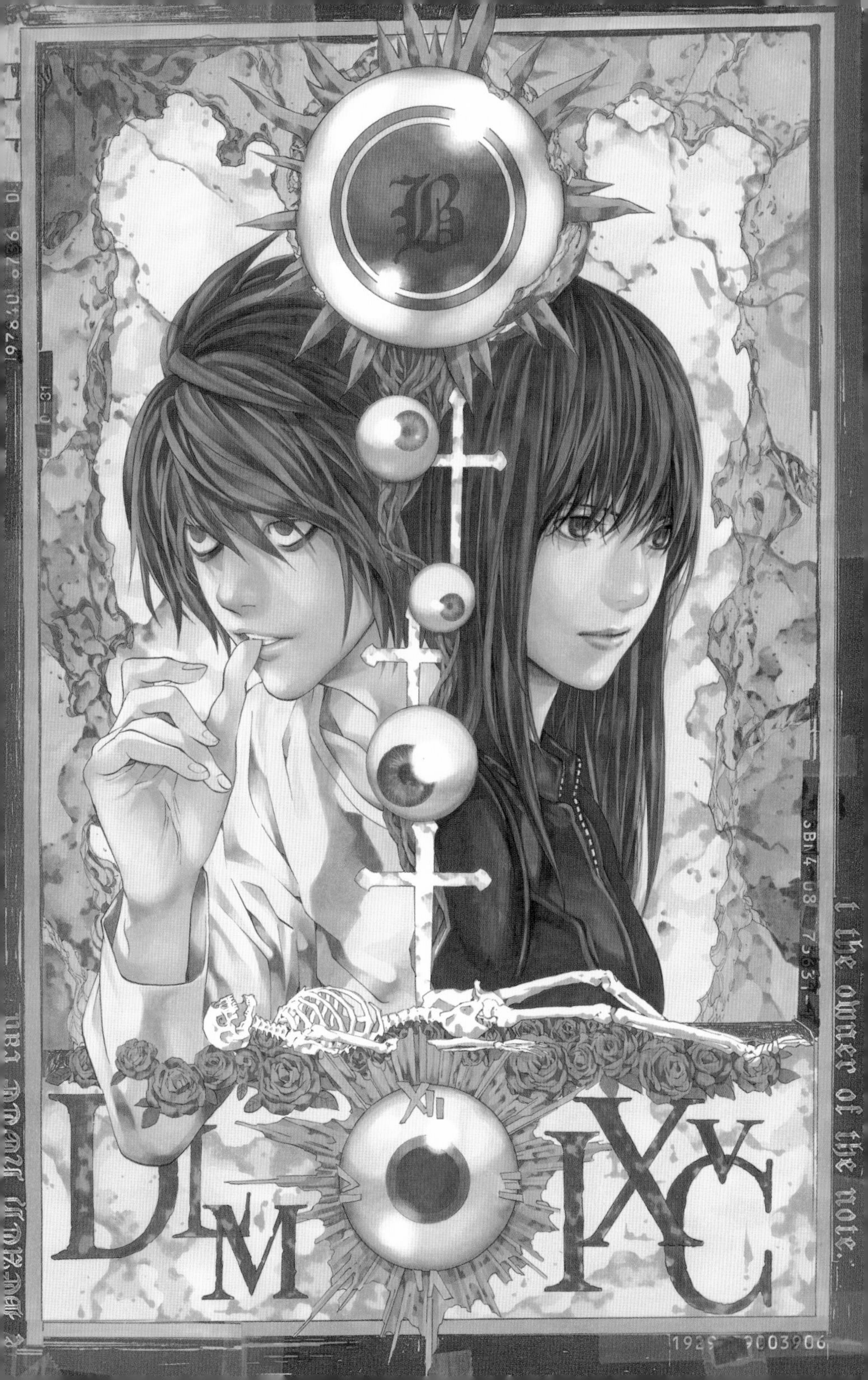

B
the owner of the note.

DEATH NOTE
ANOTHER NOTE
THE LOS ANGELES BB MURDER CASES

ORIGINAL CONCEPT BY TSUGUMI OHBA + TAKESHI OBATA

BY NISIOISIN
TRANSLATED BY ANDREW CUNNINGHAM

VIZ MEDIA
SAN FRANCISCO

DEATH NOTE – ANOTHER NOTE LOS ANGELES BB RENZOKU SATSUJIN JIKEN –
© 2006 by NISIO ISIN, Tsugumi Ohba, Takeshi Obata

Art by Takeshi Obata
Original cover and interior design by Akira Saito, Miyuki Yamaguchi [Veia]

Interior design by Courtney Utt
English translation © VIZ Media, LLC

Published by
VIZ Media, LLC
295 Bay St.
San Francisco, CA 94133

www.viz.com

Library of Congress Cataloging-in-Publication Data

Nishio, Ishin, 1981-
  [Death note. English]
  Death note : another note, the Los Angeles BB murder cases / by Nisioisin ; translated by Andrew
Cunningham.
    p. cm.
  Original concept byTsugumi Ohba and Takeshi Obata. Cf. T.p. verso.
  "First published in Japan in 2006 by Shueisha ... Tokyo"--T.p. verso.
  ISBN-13: 978-1-4215-1883-1
  ISBN-10: 1-4215-1883-X
  I. Cunningham, Andrew, 1979- II. Ohba, Tsugumi. III. Obata, Takeshi, 1969- IV. Title. V. Title: Los
Angeles BB murder cases.
  PL873.5.I84D4313 2008
  895.6'36--dc22
                          2007026102

The rights of the author of the work in this publication to be so identified have been asserted in
accordance with the Copyright, Designs and Patents Act 1988. A CIP catalogue record for this book is
available from the British Library.

Printed in China

First printing, February 2008
Fourth printing, October 2009

INDEX

Cast of Characters

L	Detective
Naomi Misora	FBI Agent
Beyond Birthday	Killer
Raye Penber	FBI Agent
Believe Bridesmaid	Victim 1
Quarter Queen	Victim 2
Backyard Bottomslash	Victim 3

"The third proved problematic. Until the case reached its end, I was reduced to nothing but an absent gaze. Think of it this way: I was a pair of abstract eyes walking around wearing my flesh as a disguise. Living as such, there was no point in expecting any form of societal responsibility or human reaction."

—Kiyoshi Kasai, Bye-bye Angel

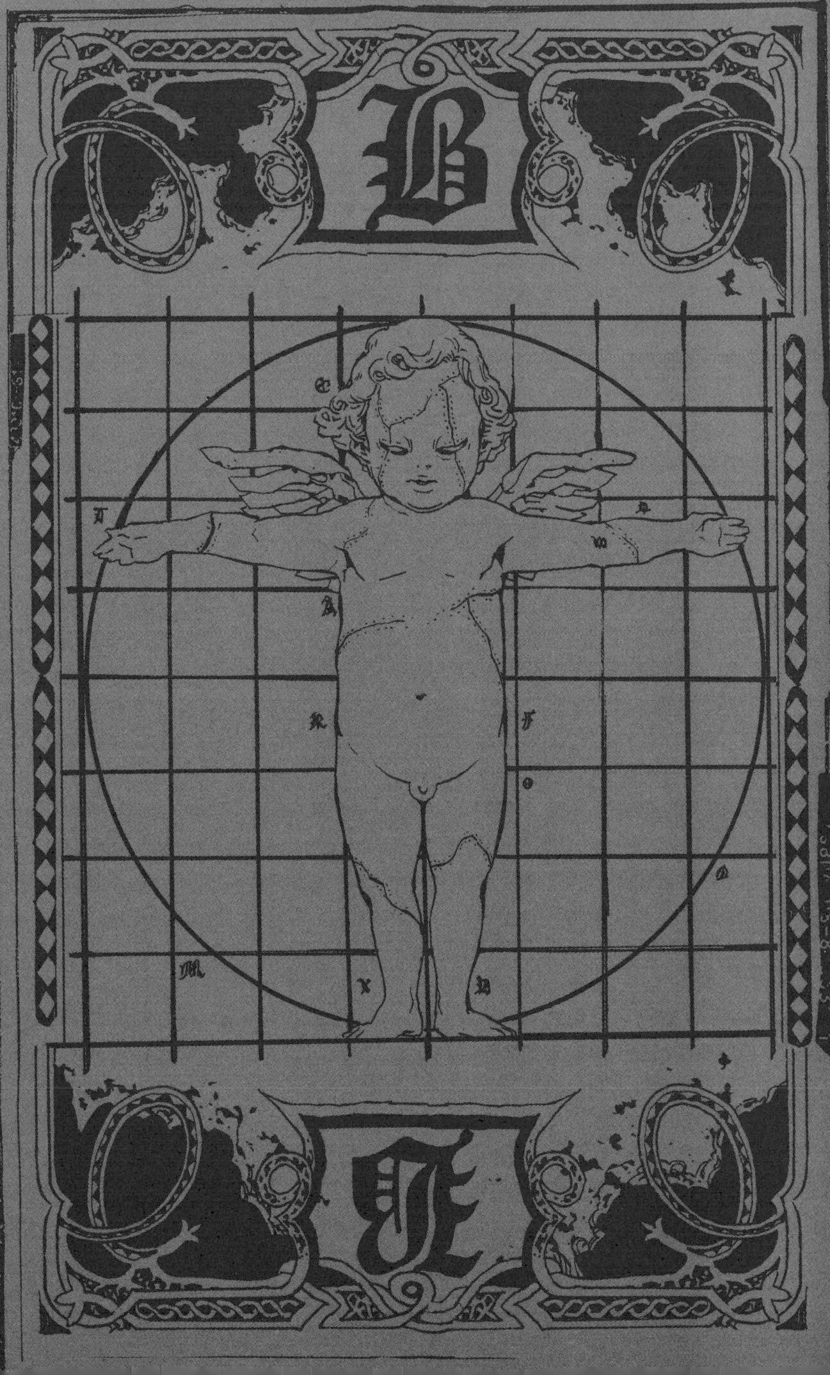
B
E

When Beyond Birthday committed his third murder, he attempted an experiment. Namely, to see if it were possible for a human being to die of internal hemorrhaging without rupturing any organs. Specifically, he drugged his victim so they fell unconscious, tied them up, and proceeded to beat their left arm thoroughly, being careful not to break the skin. He was hoping to bring about enough hemorrhaging to cause death from loss of blood, but this attempt ended, sadly, in failure. Blood congested in the arm and it turned purplish red beneath the skin, but the victim did not die. They simply shook, convulsed, and remained alive. He had been convinced the blood loss incurred by this would be enough to kill someone, but apparently he had underestimated the matter. As far as Beyond Birthday was concerned, the actual method of murder rated fairly low on the amusement scale, and it was never more than an interesting experiment. It did not particularly matter to him whether it succeeded or not. Beyond Birthday simply shrugged, and took out a knife...

No, no, no, no, no.

Not this style, not this narrative voice—I'll never manage to keep up this arch tone all the way through. The harder I try, the more bored I'll get and the lazier the writing will be. To put it in terms Holden Caulfield (one of history's most famous literary bullshitters) might use, detailing what Beyond Birthday did and thought does not suit my purposes (even if, in my position, I have a great deal of sympathy for him). Explaining the entirety of his murders in carefully phrased sentences does not in any way increase the value of these notes. This is not a report, nor is it a novel. Even if it happens to turn into one of those, I will not be happy. I hate to use such a hackneyed line, but I imagine that by the time anyone lays eyes on these words I will no longer be alive.

I hardly need to remind the reader about the epic battle between the century's greatest detective, L, and that grotesque murderer, Kira. The instrument of death was a little bit more fantastic than a guillotine (for example), but all Kira accomplished was another reign of terror and a pathetically infantile way of thinking. Looking back, I can only surmise that the gods of victory smiled on Kira for their own vain amusement. Perhaps these gods actually wanted a blood-soaked world of betrayal and false accusation. Perhaps the entire episode exists as a lesson to teach us the difference between the Almighty and the shinigami. Who knows? I, for one, have no intention of wasting any more time thinking about this most negative series of events.

To hell with Kira.

What matters to me is L.

L.

The century's greatest detective. In light of his staggering mental abilities, L died an unjust and untimely death. In the public record alone he solved over 3,500 difficult crimes, and sent three times that number of degenerates to prison. He wielded incredible power, was able to mobilize every investigative bureau in the entire world, and was applauded generously for his efforts. And during it all, he never showed his face. I want to record his words as accurately as possible. And I want to leave them for someone to find. As someone who was given the chance to follow in his footsteps...Well, I may not have been able to succeed him, but I want to leave this behind.

So what you're reading now are my notes about L. It's a dying message, not from me, and not directed at the world. The person who will most likely read this first will probably be that big-headed twit Near. But if that's the case, I will not tell him to shred or burn these pages. If it causes him pain to discover that I knew things about L that he did not, then that's fine. There's also a chance that Kira might read this…and I hope he does. If these notes tell the murderer, who only got by with the help of a supernatural killing notebook and an idiot of a shinigami, that he was, under any other circumstances, not even worth the dirt beneath L's shoes, then they have served their purpose.

I am one of the few people who ever met L as L. When and how I met him…this is the single most valuable memory I have, and I will not write it here, but on that occasion L related to me three stories of his exploits, and the episode involving Beyond Birthday was one of these. If I drop the pretense and simply refer to it as the Los Angeles BB Murder Cases, then I imagine many of you will have heard of them. Obviously, it never came to light that L—and more importantly, Wammy's House, which raised me until I was fifteen— was deeply connected to the matter, but in fact, they were. L, on principle, never got involved in a case unless there were more than ten victims or a million dollars at stake, and this is the real reason why he belatedly, but aggressively, involved himself in this little case, which only ever had three or four victims. I will explain further in the pages that follow, but for this reason, the case of the Los Angeles BB murders are a watershed event for L, for me, and even for Kira. It was a monumental event for all of us.

Why?

Because this case is where L first introduced himself as Ryuzaki.

So let us skip past all tedious descriptions of what Beyond Birthday thought, of how he went about killing his third victim, since I have no interest in that at all, and while we're at it, let's skip the second and first victims, make no effort to look back at the earlier murders, and adjust the clock's hands to the morning of the day after, the glittering moment when the century's greatest detective, L, first began to investigate the case. Oh, I almost forgot. In the event that anyone besides big-headed Near or the deluded murderer is reading these notes, then I should at least perform the basic courtesy of introducing myself, here at the end of the prologue. I am your narrator, your navigator, your storyteller. For anyone else but those two, my identity may be of no interest, but I am the old world's runner-up, the best dresser that died like a dog, Mihael Keehl. I once called myself Mello and was addressed by that name, but that was a long time ago.

Good memories and nightmares.

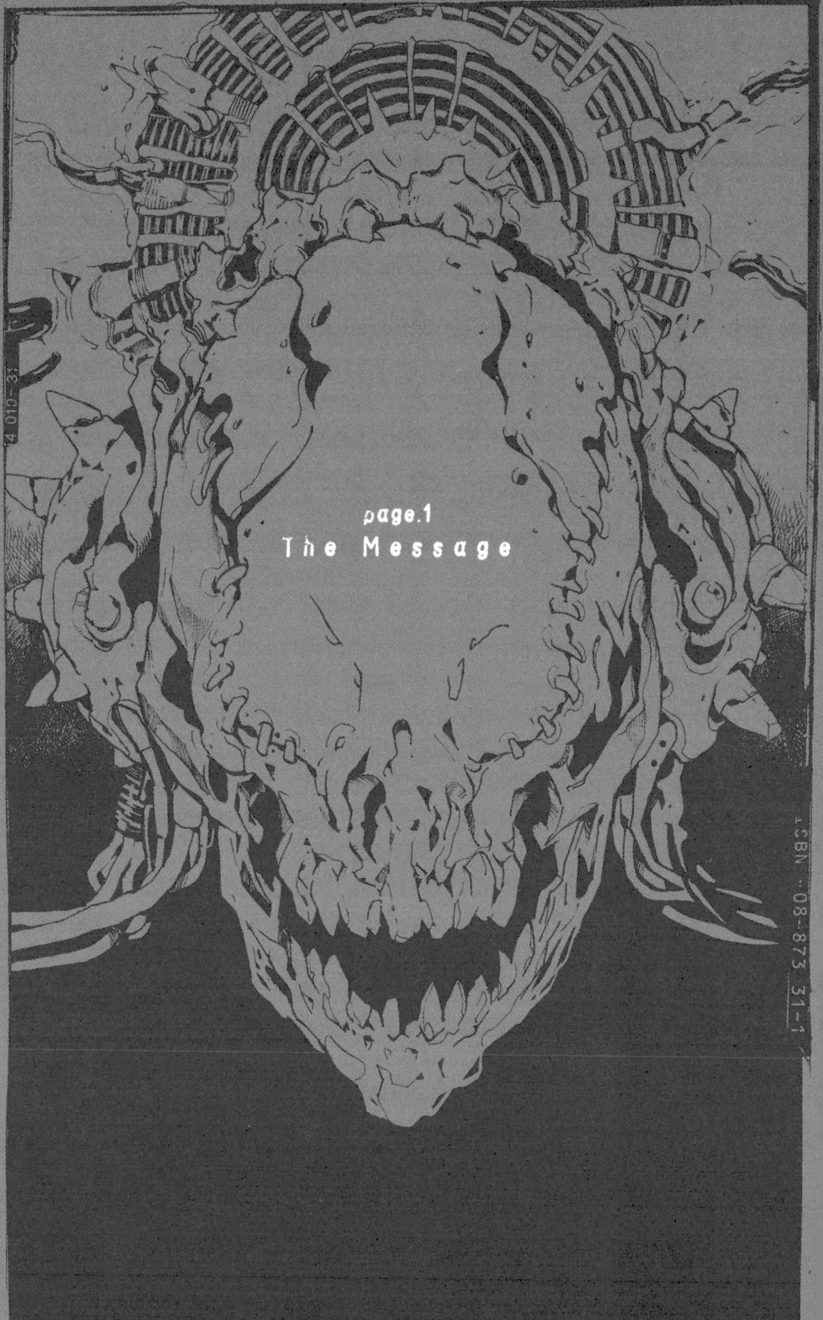
page.1
The Message

While it is now referred to as the Los Angeles BB Murder Cases—a rather catchy title—when it was actually happening, right in the middle of the whirlpool, it was never called anything so impressive. The media called it the Wara Ningyo Murders, or the L.A. Serial Locked Room Killings, or all kinds of other ghastly names. This fact was undoubtedly a source of great annoyance to Beyond Birthday—the perpetrator of the murders in question—but frankly, I think those names provide a more accurate description of what was actually happening. Either way, the day after Beyond Birthday carried out the third of the murders, August 14, 2002, 8:15 a.m. local time, the FBI agent Naomi Misora was lying dazedly on the bed in her apartment, having just woken up. She was wearing dark leather pants and a matching leather jacket, but it would be a mistake to assume she customarily slept in this outfit. She had spent several hours racing around on her motorcycle the night before, in a vain effort to burn off stress, and when she finally returned to her apartment she had fallen instantly into a sound slumber without bothering to shower or undress. Much like the name of the case, Misora has now entered the public consciousness as the one who eventually cracked the Los Angeles BB Murder Cases, but the truth is that when these events were unfolding in real time, she had been suspended from her duties as an FBI agent. According to the official records she was just on a leave of absence, but this is purely because she had absolutely no ability whatsoever to stand up to the pressure from her superiors and colleagues. Suspension, leave, summer vacation. I don't think we need to go into the reasons for her suspension here. What is certain is that this was America, she was Japanese, female, very good at her job, and the FBI is a large organization…which ought to be enough information. Obviously, she did have colleagues who had a high opinion of her, which is exactly why she had been able to work in the organization so far, but a month before, just before the Los Angeles BB murders, Misora had made a major blunder, so major even she could not believe it—which led directly to her current situation. This was not the kind of problem that could be alleviated by racing around in the middle of the night on a motorcycle.

Misora was seriously considering quitting the FBI, casting off her entire life, and moving back to Japan. Obviously, part of her was sick and tired of all the nonsense that came with the job, but even more than that was the guilt she felt over her own mistake, which hung upon her shoulders like a dead weight. Even if there had been no pressure from those around her—not that this hypothetical was even remotely possible—Misora would have asked for time off herself.

Or even resigned.

Misora slowly peeled herself off the bed, intending to shower away the sweat of the night before, but then she noticed the laptop on her desk was, for some reason, turned on. She had no recollection of turning it on—after all, she had just woken up. Had she hit the switch on her way in last night? And then fallen asleep without shutting it down again? She didn't remember doing that, but since the screen saver was working, there seemed to be no other explanation. One would assume that if she had enough energy left to turn on her computer, she would have had enough energy to undress. Misora peeled off her jacket and pants, and with her body feeling much lighter, got off the bed, moved over to her desk, and jiggled the mouse. This was enough to clear the screen saver, but at this point Misora became even more confused. The main e-mail program was running and flashing a "new mail" message. It was possible she'd fallen asleep with her computer on, but to fall asleep in the middle of checking her e-mail? While she was still wondering about that, she clicked on her inbox. There was one new message, from Raye Penber. This was the name of Misora's current boyfriend, also an FBI agent. He was the most obvious example of the agents who had a high opinion of her (not that this stopped him from begging her to transfer to a less dangerous department every time something happened). Since her leave was almost over, this might well be just business, so Misora went ahead and opened the message...

Naomi Misora-sama

I apologize for contacting you like this.

I would like to request your help in solving a certain case. If you are willing to assist me, please access the third block of the third section of the Funny Dish server on August 14th at nine a.m. The line will be open for exactly five minutes (please break through the firewall yourself).

L

PS: In order to contact you, I took the liberty of borrowing your friend's address. This was the simplest and safest way to contact you, so please forgive me. Regardless of whether you agree to help me or not, I need you to destroy this computer within twenty-four hours of reading this message.

" …"

When she finished reading, Misora immediately reread the entire message and finally checked the sender's name again.

L.

She might be suspended, but she was still an FBI agent, and obviously she recognized the name—it would have been unforgivable had she not. She briefly considered the idea that Raye Penber, or someone else, was playing a practical joke on her, but she found it hard to believe anyone would be so bold to sign their name as such. L never revealed himself in public or in private, but Misora had heard several horror stories about what had happened to detectives who had tried passing themselves off as L. It was safe to say that no one would dare use his name, even in jest.

So.

"Aw, dang," she grumbled, and proceeded to take her shower, washing away the exhaustion of the night before. She dried her long black hair and drank a cup of hot coffee.

But she was only pretending to consider the matter—she did not really have a choice. No FBI agent, particularly a low-ranking one, could ever consider turning down a request from L. But at this time Misora did not have a particularly favorable opinion of the great detective L, so she had to pretend to hesitate, if only to make herself feel better. If you consider Misora's personality, the reasons for this are clear. It seemed obvious that the reason her laptop had been turned on was that L had hacked it, and she was more than a little depressed that she would now have to randomly destroy the new computer she had just purchased a month before.

"I don't mind…I mean, I do, but…"

She didn't have a choice.

At just past 8:50, Misora sat down in front of her laptop, which now had less than twenty-three hours left to live, and began following L's instructions. She was not an expert hacker, but she had been taught the basics as part of her FBI training.

Just as she successfully gained access to the server, her entire screen went white. Misora was momentarily alarmed, but then she noticed a giant calligraphic L floating in the center of the screen, and relaxed.

"Naomi Misora," came a voice from the laptop speakers, after a brief pause. It was obviously a synthetic voice. But this was the voice recognized as L's by every investigative department in the world. Misora had heard it several times before—but this was the first time it had ever addressed her directly. It felt weird, like she was hearing her name on TV—not that she had ever had that experience, but this was what she imagined it would be like.

"This is L."

"Hi," Misora started to say, but then realized how pointless that was. Her laptop did not have a microphone installed, and there was no way for him to hear her.

Instead, she typed in, "This is Naomi Misora. It's an honor to speak to you, L." If her connection was sound, he should be able to receive this.

"Naomi Misora, are you familiar with the murder investigation going on in Los Angeles as we speak?"

L got right down to business, without acknowledging her words at all. Presumably this was because he had to complete this communication by 9:05, but his manner and attitude rubbed Misora the wrong way. Like it was a given that she would cooperate with him— which was true, but acting like it showed no respect for her pride. Misora allowed herself to bang on the keyboard rather loudly.

"I am not so skilled that I can keep track of all the murder investigations happening in Los Angeles."

"Oh? I am."

He'd returned her sarcasm with a boast.

L continued, "I'm referring to the serial killings—the third victim was found yesterday. I believe there will be more victims to come. HNN news is calling it the Wara Ningyo Murders."

"The Wara Ningyo Murders?"

She had not heard about it. She was on leave and had been deliberately avoiding that kind of news. Misora had lived in Japan until she graduated high school and was familiar with the term, but hearing it pronounced in English gave it an edge of unfamiliarity.

"I would like to solve this case," L said. "I need to arrest the killer. But your help in this matter is vital, Naomi Misora."

"Why me?" she typed. This could be taken to mean either "Why do you need my help?" or "Why should I help you?" but L took the first meaning without a moment's hesitation. Sarcasm appeared to be lost on him.

"Naturally, because you are a skilled investigator, Naomi Misora."

"I'm on a leave of absence…"

"I know. Isn't that convenient?"

Three victims, he'd said.

Obviously, it depended on the victims, but from what L had told her this case had not yet reached the kind of scale required for the FBI to get involved. She would normally have assumed that this was why he had approached her instead of going through the FBI director, but this was much too sudden. And she had been given almost no time to think things through. But it had been enough time for her to wonder why L would be involved in a case too small for the FBI to notice. She did not imagine he would answer that question over her computer, however.

She glanced at her clock.

She had one more minute.

"Okay. I'll help in any way I can," Misora typed.

L answered instantly, "Thank you. I knew you would agree."

He did not sound very thankful.

But perhaps that could be blamed on the synthetic nature of his voice.

"Let me explain how you will contact me in the future. We have no time, so I will be brief. First..."

First, she had to know the basic details of the Los Angeles BB Murder Cases. On July 31st, 2002, in the bedroom of a small house on Hollywood's Insist Street, a man named Believe Bridesmaid was killed. He lived alone, working as a freelance writer. He had written articles for dozens of magazines under many different names and was relatively well known in the industry—which means exactly nothing, but in this case appears to have been fairly accurate. He was strangled. He was first knocked out with some sort of drug and then strangled from behind with some sort of string. There were no signs of struggle—all things considered, a smoothly executed crime. The second murder occurred four days later, on August 4th, 2002. This time it was downtown, in an apartment on Third Avenue, and the victim was a female named Quarter Queen. This time the victim was beaten to death, her skull caved in from the front by something long and hard. Once again, the victim appeared to have been drugged first and was unconscious at the time of death. As for why it was determined that these two murders were committed by the same killer...well, anyone who saw the scene of the crime instantly noticed the connection.

There were straw voodoo dolls nailed to the walls at both places. These dolls were specifically known as Wara Ningyo.

Four of them on Insist Street.

Three of them on Third Avenue.

Nailed to the walls.

The Wara Ningyo had been covered in the news, so strictly speaking there was a chance of a copycat crime, but several other details matched as well, leading the police to begin treating the case as a serial killing. But if that was the case, that left a very big question—there was absolutely nothing to connect Believe Bridesmaid with Quarter Queen. Neither one of them had the other's number in their cell phones, neither one of them had the other's card in their business card holder, and besides, Quarter Queen did not own a cell phone or a business card holder—she was a thirteen-year-old girl. What connection could she possibly have to a forty-four-year-old professional freelance writer? If there was a connection, it was probably through the girl's mother, who was out of town when the murder happened, but given the difference in neighborhoods and situations between the two, it was still difficult to see any significant connection. To use a term from an old-fashioned detective novel, there was a missing link—they could not find any connection between the victims. The investigation had naturally focused on this, but nine days later (by which time the media had begun calling them the Wara Ningyo Murders) on August 13th, 2002, the third murder happened.

There were two Wara Ningyo on the wall.

There was one less doll with each murder.

The third murder was in West L.A., in a townhouse near the Metrorail Glass Station, and the victim's name was Backyard Bottomslash. This victim was another female—age twenty-six, midway between the first and second victims—and she was a bank clerk. Once again, she had no connections with Believe Bridesmaid or Quarter Queen at all. It seemed unlikely they had even bumped into each other on the street. She died from loss of blood—massive hemorrhaging. Strangulation, beating, and finally stabbing—each time a different method of murder, giving the unnatural impression that he was trying something new with each killing. And he left no useful clues at any of the scenes. The only other thing to investigate was the link between them, but since none was found—which was very strange for murders of this type—the third murder left the police at a complete loss. The killer was far better at this than the police were. I have no intention of praising Beyond Birthday, but in this case I will give him the credit he is due.

Oh, right—in addition to the Wara Ningyo, there was one other major similarity between the scenes—they were all locked rooms. Just like an old mystery novel. The detectives investigating the case had not put a lot of value on this particular aspect of the case...but when Naomi Misora received the file on the case from L, this word was the first thing that caught her attention.

When Misora began investigating the case—not as an FBI agent, but as an individual under L's supervision—it was the day after she received L's request, August 15th. She was off duty, so her badge and gun had been taken away from her, leaving her with no more rights or weaponry than any ordinary citizen.

But she did not particularly mind—Misora had never been the kind of agent to throw her authority around. She was a little put out, and her mental condition was a little choppy, so she was not in the best condition to tackle the case, but in that sense her emotional state was similar to L's own. In other words, she was not good at working in groups, and her ability shone brightest when she escaped the bindings of organizations and worked on her own—which in turn might explain why she had a pinch of resentment coloring her feelings toward L.

But on August 15th, at just past noon, Naomi Misora was on Hollywood's Insist Street, the scene of the first murder. Looking up at the house, which seemed a trifle large for a man who lived alone, Misora reached into her bag, took out a cell phone, and dialed the number she'd been given. She had been told it was scrambled five-fold and completely safe. Not only safe for L, but also safe for the off-duty Misora.

"L, I've reached the scene."

"Good," the artificial voice said, as if he'd been waiting for her.

Misora briefly wondered where L was, in what kind of environment he went about his investigations, but she quickly realized that it made no difference either way.

"What should I do?"

"Naomi Misora, are you inside the building or outside?"

"Outside. I'm headed toward the scene of the crime but have not yet entered the yard."

"Then please go inside. It should be unlocked. I've arranged for that."

"Thanks."

Well prepared.

She grit her teeth, resisting the urge to say something sarcastic. Normally she would have considered being prepared a point worth respecting, but she found it hard to accept that anyone was *this* thoroughly prepared.

She opened the door and entered the house. The victim had been killed in his bedroom, and Misora had been involved in enough investigations with the FBI to make a fair guess at where that room was located from the outside. A house like this usually had the bedroom on the first floor, so she moved accordingly. It'd been two weeks since the murder, but they were obviously keeping the place clean. There wasn't a speck of dust anywhere.

"But, L…"

"What?"

"According to the data I received yesterday—not to state the obvious, but the police have already examined the scene."

"Yes."

"I'm not sure how you did it, but you already have the police reports covering that."

"Yes."

"…"

Not very helpful.

"So there's no point in my being here?"

"No," L said. "I expect you will be able to find something that the police did not."

"Well…that's clear enough."

Or perhaps a tad obvious.

It ultimately explained nothing.

"They say you should visit the crime scene a hundred times, so going there is hardly pointless. Some time has passed, so it's possible something floated to the surface. Naomi Misora, the first thing we need to think about in this case is the connection between the victims. What links Believe Bridesmaid, Quarter Queen, and the new victim, Backyard Bottomslash? Or is there no connection, and these murders are completely random? But even if they are random, there must be some logic by which the killer selects his victims. What I am asking you to do, Naomi Misora, is to discover this missing link."

"I see…"

She didn't really, but she had begun to understand that arguing with L would not make him stop being evasive and tell her what she actually wanted to know, so she decided to not ask many questions. Besides, she had found the bedroom. The door opened inward and had a thumb turn lock.

A locked room.

The second and third crime scenes also had thumb turn locks… was that a link? No, that much information had been in the file. The police had already noticed it. L was looking for something more.

It was not a very large room, but there was not much furniture, so it did not feel cramped. There was a big bed in the center of the space, but the only other furniture were a few bookshelves. These shelves were mainly filled with how-to books for different leisure activities and famous Japanese comics, suggesting that Believe Bridesmaid had used this room exclusively for relaxation. He seemed to be the type to carefully separate work and private time—not a type often found in freelance writers. Presumably there was a study of some kind on the second floor, Misora thought, absently glancing up at the ceiling. She would have to check there later.

"By the way, Naomi Misora. What are your thoughts on the culprit behind these killings? I'd like to hear your current thinking on the matter."

"I doubt if my thoughts will be of any use to you, L…"

"All thoughts are of use."

"…"

Oh?

Misora thought for a moment.

"He's abnormal," she replied, not bothering to choose her words, but just stating her mind. This was the main impression she had received the day before, reading over the file. "Not just because he's killed three people, but…each action he took just drove that impression home. And he's not even trying to hide it."

"For example?"

"For example…fingerprints. They have not found a single fingerprint at any of the crime scenes. They had been wiped away completely."

"True…but Naomi Misora, surely leaving no fingerprints is the most basic of criminal techniques."

"Not to this extent," Misora said, annoyed—she knew L understood what she was driving at and was sure that he was testing her ability, no matter what he said. Testing to see if she was capable of serving as his man on the scene. "If you didn't want to leave fingerprints, most people would wear gloves—or otherwise, wipe down anything they touched. But this guy…apparently he wiped clean *every fingerprint in the house*. At all three scenes. At first I wondered if he'd been to the victim's house so many times he had no idea what he'd touched and what he hadn't, but once I read that he had unscrewed the lightbulbs and *wiped the sockets*, it became a completely different story. What else can you call that but abnormal?"

"I agree."

" … "

Did he, now?

"So, L, back to what I was saying earlier, if he's taken such extreme precautions, then I doubt I'm going to be able to find anything new here. It's a faint hope at best. Someone like this isn't going to make a mistake."

A mistake.

Like the one she'd made last month.

"Normally this kind of investigation starts by finding the criminal's mistake, and then filling in the puzzle from there, but in this case, I doubt we'll find anything like that."

"No, I don't think we will," L said. "But *what if it isn't a mistake?*"

"Not a mistake?"

"Yes. Something he *deliberately left behind*. And if the police detectives simply failed to notice it…then we might have a chance."

" … "

Deliberately leaving clues? Did that *ever* happen? Not in the normal run of things, no—why would anyone leave something behind that could be used against them? Or wait. Now that he mentioned it, they already knew two examples of exactly that behavior. One was the Wara Ningyo nailed to the walls, and the other was the thumb turn locks, creating a locked room. These were not mistakes, but had clearly been left behind by the killer. Especially the latter. Exactly the thing that Misora had been most interested in—locked rooms were almost always created when the killer was trying to make it look like a suicide. But the first victim was strangled from behind, the second was beaten to death with a weapon that was not found at the scene, and the third victim was stabbed with, again, a weapon not left at the scene…none of which could ever be mistaken for a suicide. Which meant there was nothing to be gained from creating a locked room. It was not a mistake, but it was unnatural.

The Wara Ningyo were the same.

She had no idea what they meant.

Since Wara Ningyo were used for curses in Japan, there were people wildly theorizing that the killer was Japanese, or someone with a deep-seated grudge against the Japanese, but especially since these Wara Ningyo were a particularly cheap variety that could be easily purchased in any toy shop (for about three dollars) no one theory had gained prominence.

Misora shut the door behind her, and since the thumb turn lock was at waist height, she absently turned it and locked herself in. Then she checked each location where the dolls had been nailed to the walls.

There had been four of them.

One on each of the four walls of the square room. Obviously, they had been taken away by the police as critical evidence, and were no longer here. It was easy enough to tell where they had been, since there were holes in the walls. Misora took six pictures out of her bag. One of each of the four dolls. One showed the victim, Believe Bridesmaid, lying on his back on the bed. It clearly showed the rope marks around his neck.

And then the last picture.

This was not from the scene, but a close up of Believe Bridesmaid's bare chest, taken during the autopsy. There were a number of major cuts on it, which appeared to have been carved into his flesh with a knife. They were not that deep, but ran in all directions. According to the report, they had been made after the victim's death.

"Generally speaking, when the killer engages in this sort of meaningless destruction of the corpse, they have a deep-seated grudge against their victim...for a freelance writer who would take any job, I wouldn't be surprised if he had quite a few enemies. He did a lot of gossip columns…"

"But Naomi Misora, that does not explain the connection to the second and third murders. Both of those bodies were also damaged in ways that had no direct connection to the cause of death—in fact, the damage seems to have escalated with each murder."

"It's possible Bridesmaid was the only one he had a grudge against, and the other two murders were designed to disguise that. Or maybe it wasn't Bridesmaid, but one of the other two…or two out of the three, and the third was camouflage. The destruction might be getting worse because it's part of the disguise, or…"

"You believe the killer is only *pretending* to kill indiscriminately?"

"No. This is just one pattern worth considering. This idea would explain the Wara Ningyo. I mean, maybe he deliberately left them there to prove that all three were killed by the same man—and the locked doors might be for the same reason."

In which case moving from Hollywood to downtown to the west side of town could be seen as an effort to confuse the investigation. The more people the case connected to, the more chaotic the investigation would become…and the selection of a young girl as the second victim may have been done deliberately to make him look like a psycho.

"Pretending to be abnormal…well, just the idea of doing that is abnormal enough," L said. Misora was surprised to hear him express such a human sentiment. The emotion she felt was very similar to being impressed, and she quickly put the conversation back on topic—to cover her reaction, if not to hide it.

"So, L, I feel ridiculous trying to figure out a connection between the victims. I think the police are doing a fine job with that, and… frankly, checking out everyone who knew each of them seems more useful. I mean, the third victim, Backyard Bottomslash…she must have been involved in all kinds of business dealings at the bank."

"But Naomi Misora," L interrupted. "This is no time for idle musings. I believe there will be a fourth murder in the near future."

"Mmm…"

He'd said something similar the day before. That there would be more victims. But based on what? With the killer still at large, it was an obvious possibility, but it seemed just as likely the murders would end at three. It all depended on the killer's whim—as an investigator, she found it hard to place the odds higher than fifty-fifty.

"The number of Wara Ningyo," L said. "Four where you are, three downtown with the second victim, and two at the third scene, in West L.A.—one less doll at each scene."

"Yeah. So?"

"The number of dolls can still decrease by one."

"…"

She should have guessed. In fact, it made little sense to count backward from four to two and then stop. Even if Misora's theory was right, and he was killing indiscriminately to camouflage his real victim, then the more victims the more effective this plan would be. Of course, each new murder was an added risk, but the return probably justified it. Frankly, there was no way of telling if this killer even considered murders a risk—there were certainly some killers who considered the murders themselves return enough. And it was abnormal to pretend to be abnormal…

"So, L…you think there will be as many as two additional murders?"

"More than a ninety percent chance," he said. "I'd say a hundred, but there is a small possibility that something will happen on the killer's side, preventing him from continuing. So maybe ninety-two percent. But Misora, if something does happen, it will not be two more—only one. There's only a thirty percent chance of a fifth murder."

"Thirty percent?"

Quite a drop.

"Why? There are two more Wara Ningyo...and if he's using the dolls to represent his victims..."

"But in that case, *he won't be able to leave a Wara Ningyo at the fifth crime scene.* He will go from two dolls to one when he kills the fourth victim. That doll will make it obvious that these are the work of the same killer, but..."

"Oh! I see," Misora said, wincing at her own stupidity. Obviously, whatever the killer's motive, leaving a Wara Ningyo at the scene was part of his rules. He would hardly kill a fifth victim when the number of dolls had reached zero.

"There is a thirty percent chance the killer won't think things through that far, but that's extremely doubtful. After all, he did wipe the lightbulb sockets..."

"So there will only be four victims total. The next one is the last."

"No. The third was the last," L said firmly. Despite being a synthetic voice. "There will not be another. Not with me involved."

"..."

Confidence?

Or hubris?

Neither one was something Misora had laid claim to for a while now. The last few weeks in particular.

What had confidence been like?

What had pride been like?

Misora no longer knew.

"But I need your assistance, Naomi Misora. I expect great things from your investigations."

"Do you?"

"Yes. Please keep your heart frozen while you work. In my experience, what a case like this needs most is a mind that will not be moved by anything. Behave as if you are playing chess on the ice."

"..."

Wasn't that called curling?

"L, you do know that I'm on a leave of absence?"

"Yes. That's why I asked you for help. With this case, I need a skilled individual who can work on their own."

"So I imagine you also know *why* I'm on a leave of absence?"

"No," he said, to Misora's surprise. "I don't know that."

"You didn't check?"

"I wasn't interested. You are skilled, and were currently available, and that was all that mattered—unless there was something I should know about? In that case, I could find out in under a minute."

"No…" she said, grimacing.

She had felt like the entire world knew about her blunder, but not even the world's greatest detective knew. And he had described Misora's leave of absence/suspension as making her "available." She had never thought to wonder, but it seemed L did have a sense of humor.

"Okay, L, if we're going to stop the fourth murder, we should begin. What should I do first?"

"What can you do?"

"I can do what I can do," Misora said. "I know I keep asking, but if I'm going to look over the scene again…searching for anything he left behind besides the Wara Ningyo…what, specifically, am I looking for?"

"Any kind of message."

"Message?"

"Yes. This was not listed in the data I gave you, but nine days before July 31st, before the first murder, on July 22nd, the LAPD received a letter."

"A letter?"

Where was this going?

The LAPD…?

"Connected to the case?"

"At the moment, none of the detectives involved have noticed a connection. I don't know for certain if there actually is one, but I think there is."

"What percent?"

"Eighty percent."

Instant response.

"The sender is unknown—a forwarding system was used, and there's no way to tell where it was sent from. Inside the envelope was a single piece of paper with a crossword puzzle written on it."

"A crossword puzzle? Hunh…"

"Don't be dismissive. It was a very difficult puzzle, and no one could solve it. Of course, we could also take that to mean no one applied themselves to it seriously, but it seems reasonable to hypothesize that several policemen working together were unable to solve the puzzle."

"I see. So?"

"Eventually they decided the puzzle was just a prank, and it was thrown away…but my information-gathering network acquired a copy through other channels yesterday."

"Yesterday…"

So that was why it wasn't in the file. Even as Misora was preparing to start her investigation, L had been pursuing the matter from a different angle.

"I solved it," L said.

Apparently that hypothesis about the difficulty of the puzzle had been a preemptive form of bragging. He must get frowned at a lot, Misora thought. Not that she was one to talk.

"If I'm not mistaken, then the answer to that puzzle is where you are—*the address of the first murder.*"

"221 Insist St., Hollywood? *Where I am now?* But that means…then…"

"Exactly. He told them he was going to commit these murders.

But since the puzzle was so difficult that no one could solve it, it did not realistically stand a chance of serving that purpose…"

"Has the LAPD received any other letters like that? Indicating the address for the second or third murders?"

"No. I checked the entire state of California, just to be sure. I have discovered no other such letters or e-mails. I plan to keep looking, but…"

"Then it might just be a coincidence? No, that's impossible. If it listed the address exactly, it must be…so why nine days before?"

"The time between the second and third murders was also nine days. August 4th to August 13th. It's possible the killer likes the number nine."

"But there are only four days between the first and second murders…pure chance?"

"A reasonable interpretation. But it seems worth remembering that time lag. Nine days, four days, nine days. Either way, the killer is the type to advertise his actions to the police. Even if he was just pretending to be that type of killer, there remains a very good chance that there is some kind of message in the room, something besides the Wara Ningyo."

"Hmm…so…"

Something deliberate.

A message much harder to understand than the Wara Ningyo… something like a very challenging crossword puzzle. Misora felt like she was at last starting to understand why L needed her help. There was no way an armchair detective would be able to find something like this on his own. You had to see the scene with your own eyes, be able to reach out and touch things…and it required quality over quantity. Someone who could look at the scene from his own perspective, his own way of thinking…

But she also thought he was putting too much stock in her. If she had to be L's eyes as well…that was too much for an ordinary

FBI agent to handle.

"Something wrong, Naomi Misora?"

"No…never mind."

"Okay. For the moment, let us cease communication. I have many things I must attend to."

"Certainly."

This was L, so he was undoubtedly solving several other difficult cases all at once. Cases all over the world. For him, this case was just one of many parallel investigations. How else could he maintain his reputation as the world's greatest detective?

The century's greatest detective, L.

The detective with no clients.

"I'll be waiting to hear good things from you. The next time you call me, please use the number five line, Naomi Misora," L said, and hung up.

Misora folded her phone and put it back in her bag. Then she moved over to the bookshelves to start her investigation. There was nothing in the bedroom but the bed and the bookshelves, so there wasn't much else to investigate.

"Not as bad as his killer, but it looks like Believe Bridesmaid was reasonably obsessive himself…"

The books were packed tightly onto the shelves with no excess space. Misora did a quick count—fifty-seven volumes. She tried to pull one out at random, but this was rather difficult to do. Her index finger alone proved inadequate, and she had to use her thumb and the lever principle to pry it out. She flipped through the pages, well aware that this was pointless. She was just keeping her hands busy while she tried to figure out what to do. It would be nice and simple if there were a message hidden between the pages of the book, but that was too much to hope for. According to the files, like the light-bulb sockets, each page of every book had been wiped, removing all fingerprints—suggesting not only that the killer was extremely finicky, but that the police had in fact gone through all of the books. One could assume there had been no messages.

Or the message had been arranged in a way the police had not noticed...something that looked like an ordinary bookmark, but actually had a code hidden on it...But after flipping through another few books, she dismissed this theory as well. The books here did not have bookmarks. Believe Bridesmaid did not appear to be the bookmark type. Many fussy readers detest the slight curve in the page a bookmark can leave.

...Which meant that even the most fastidious killer would never dream of placing anything inside a book.

Misora moved away from the shelves. She glanced down at the bed, but there seemed to be even less to investigate here. There was nothing to do but pull the sheets off and look under the mattress. And she didn't even need to check the file to know that the police had already done that. It seemed virtually impossible to hide a message on the bed that the police would not notice.

"Under the carpet...behind the wallpaper...no, no, why would he hide the message? He wants it to be found. It's not a message if it isn't found. He sent the crossword puzzle to the police...very egotistical. He wants the puzzles to be difficult...*to prove that we're stupid.*"

He wasn't trying to outwit them.

He was mocking them.

"'You are beneath me,' 'You can never beat me,'—that's what the messages are saying. Which means...he's not trying to make everything go right and avoid getting caught, he's after something more than his goals...or making fun of us is his primary goal? Who is 'us'? The police? The LAPD? Society? The U.S.A.? The world? No... the scale's too small...This is more personal. So this message...or something like a message...There must be one somewhere in this room...or, wait..."

"There must be…" was wrong.

Maybe there *wasn't*.

"Something that *should* be here, but *isn't*…something missing, that used to be here…the Wara Ningyo? No, those were a symbol for the victims, not a message…the bedroom…oh, right! The occupant! The bedroom's occupant isn't here."

Something missing, something no longer here.

Like the room's owner, Believe Bridesmaid.

Misora took out the photographs again and looked carefully at the two pictures of Bridesmaid's corpse—one taken at the scene, and one taken during the autopsy. If the killer had left a message on the body, it was obviously not the rope marks, but the knife wounds on his chest. Like Misora had said to L, normally these would be taken as a sign of a personal vendetta, but now that she thought about it, they weren't natural. In the photo from the scene, the body was on its back, wearing a T-shirt which had a few bloodstains on it…but the T-shirt itself wasn't damaged at all. Which meant that after the killer had murdered him, he had taken the T-shirt off, cut up the body with a knife, and then put the T-shirt back on. If this were a simple grudge, he would have just cut right through the fabric. Was there a reason he didn't want to damage the T-shirt? But he didn't seem to mind if it got bloodstains…and the T-shirt definitely belonged to the victim. It was one he always slept in…

"If you…look at them right…these marks…do look like letters… sort of…"

You had to twist the picture around a lot, though.

"V…C…I? No, M…another V…X? D…and that's three I's in a row…L? That looks like L…hmm…feels like I'm forcing it…"

This only worked if you were looking for it. It wasn't like kanji or Hangul—alphabet letters were constructed of simple lines and curves, and any random scratch marks, whether with a pencil or knife, would look like *something*.

"Normally I'd like to see what the detectives in charge think, the people actually involved in the case...but I don't have a badge at the moment, so that's out of the question. Of course, L's probably handling that side of things for me."

Misora was starting to appreciate how much harder it was to work on your own, without the support of the organization. She had always felt out of place in the FBI, but she was just now realizing how much she had taken advantage of the resources it offered.

"I guess I should check the other rooms...seems sort of pointless. But if he wiped all the fingerprints in the house..." she murmured, and turned to leave the room.

But then it occurred to her that there was one place she hadn't checked yet. Under the bed. Easy enough to overlook, and far more likely than under the carpet or behind the wallpaper—it seemed fairly unlikely that the police had missed such an obvious blind spot, but it seemed worth crawling under there, just to be sure. There might be something new she could see from down there. For this reason, Misora crouched down next to the bed...

"...?!"

And a hand reached out from underneath it.

Misora jumped backward instantly, forced down the surge of emotions this sudden turn of events stirred up, and put her fists up. She didn't have a gun with her—not because she was suspended, but simply because she had never really gotten used to carrying one around. With no gun, she had no trigger to pull.

"What...no, who are you?" she roared, trying to sound intimidating. But the hand was joined by a second hand, as if her voice was just the wind blowing, and a body followed it. A man, crawling out from under the bed.

How long...had he been here...?

Was he under the bed this whole time?

Had he heard her talking to L?

All kinds of questions flooded through Misora's mind.

"Answer me! Who are you?!"

She put one hand inside her jacket, pretending she had a gun. The man raised his head.

And slowly stood up.

Natural black hair.

A plain shirt, faded jeans.

He was a young man, with dark lines under his wide, bulging eyes.

Thin, and apparently fairly tall, but his back was curved, leaving his gaze two heads lower than Misora's so he appeared to be looking up at her.

"Nice to meet you," he said, completely unruffled. He bowed even lower. "Please call me Ryuzaki."

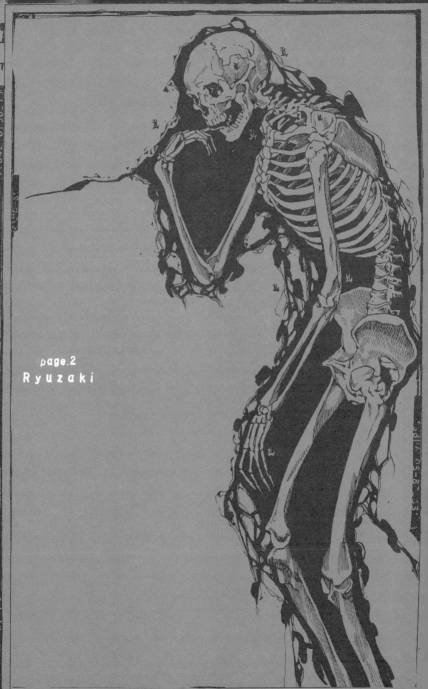

page.2
Ryuzaki

L had earned a certain degree of hostility from other detectives, and the jealous ones called him a hermit detective, or a computer detective, but neither one of these is a particularly accurate representation of the truth. Naomi Misora had also tended to think of L as an armchair detective, but in fact, L was quite the opposite, a very active, aggressive individual. While he had absolutely no interest in social conventions, he was certainly not the kind of detective to shut himself up in a dark room with the shades drawn and refuse to come out. It is now common knowledge that the three great post war detectives, L, Eraldo Coil and Danuve were all actually the same person. Certainly, anyone reading these notes is almost certain to know…though they may not know that L engaged in a war with the real Eraldo Coil, and the real Danuve, and emerged victorious, claiming their detective codes. The details of this detective war I will save for another occasion, but in addition to those three names, L possessed many other detective codes. I have no idea how many, but there were at least three digits' worth. And quite a number of those were fairly public detectives—just like, as anyone reading these notes must know, he appeared before Kira, calling himself Ryuzaki or Ryuga Hideki. Of course, Naomi Misora had no way of knowing this, but in my opinion, the name L was, for him, just one of many. He never had any direct connection to that identity, he never thought of himself as L—it was just the most famous and most powerful of the many detective codes that he used during his life. The name had its uses, but lacked obscurity. L had a real name that nobody knew, and nobody will ever know, but a name which only he knew never defined him. I sometimes wonder if L himself ever knew exactly which name was written in the Death Note, which name it was that killed him.

I wonder.

But back to the Los Angeles BB Murder Cases.

"Ryuzaki…" Naomi Misora said, looking over the black business card he had handed her without bothering to hide her suspicious. "Rue Ryuzaki, right?"

"Yes. Rue Ryuzaki," the man said, in the same unruffled tone. His wide eyes stared at her through the dark circles around them, and he nibbled at his thumbnail.

They had moved out of the bedroom into the living room of Believe Bridesmaid's house. They were sitting opposite each other on expensive sofas. Ryuzaki was seated with his knees up and his arms wrapped around them. Misora thought this looked a little childish, but since Ryuzaki was obviously not a child, it seemed a little creepy. The fact that she failed to comment on it at all was because she was much too grown up. To escape the awkward silence, Misora looked down at the card again—*Rue Ryuzaki: Detective.*

"According to this, you're a detective?"

"Yes, I am."

"You mean…a private detective?"

"No, that term would not be very accurate. I feel the word 'private' carries with it an excess of neurotic egotism…you might say that I am an unprivate detective—a detective without ego."

"I see…"

In other words, he didn't have a license.

If she'd had a pen, she would have written "idiot" on the card, but sadly, there were no writing implements within reach, so she settled for putting it down on the table as far from her as possible, as if it were unclean.

"So, Ryuzaki…let me ask again, what exactly were you doing

down there?"

"Same as you. Investigating," Ryuzaki said, without the slightest change in his expression.

His black-rimmed eyes never blinked. Rather unsettling.

"I was hired by the parents of this house's owner—by Mr. Bridesmaid's parents, and am currently conducting an investigation into the killings. It seemed to me that you were here for much the same reason, Misora."

"…"

By this point Misora no longer really cared who this Ryuzaki was—private detective or unprivate detective, she wanted nothing to do with him. The only problem was how much of her conversation he had heard from under the bed…which in a worst-case scenario could affect her future career. If any information about the mysterious L was made public because of her, she would have to do a great deal more than simply resign. She had casually broached the subject, and he had claimed that the bed muffled the sound of her voice and he had not been able to make out what she was saying, but this was not something she could afford to believe.

"Yes…I'm also a detective," Misora said, feeling like she had no other choice. If she had not been on a leave of absence, she would have claimed to be an FBI agent, but since she was, she did not want to risk him asking to see her badge. It seemed safer to lie—after all, there was a distinct possibility he was lying too. She did not need to feel at all guilty.

"I can't tell you who I'm working for, but I've been asked to investigate in secret. To find out who killed Believe Bridesmaid, Quarter Queen, and Backyard Bottomslash…"

"Have you? Then we can cooperate!" he said instantly.

Nerve on this level became oddly refreshing.

"So, Ryuzaki. Did you find anything under the bed that might prove useful in solving this case? I assume you were looking for anything the killer might have left behind, but…"

"No, nothing of the sort. I heard someone come into the house, so I decided to hide and monitor the situation. After a while it became clear that you were not a dangerous character, so I emerged."

"A dangerous character?"

"Yes. For example, the killer himself, coming back to get something he forgot. If that were the case, then what a chance! But apparently my hopes were in vain."

"…"

Liar.

She could *smell* that lie coming.

Misora was now almost completely convinced that he'd been hiding down there to listen to her conversation with L. In any other situation, this would simply be paranoia, but this Ryuzaki character was no ordinary man.

There was nothing about him that wasn't suspicious.

"However, instead I have been lucky enough to meet you, so it was not a total write off. This is not a novel or a comic book, so there is no reason for fellow detectives to despise each other. What do you say, Misora? Will you agree to an exchange of information?"

"…No. Thank you for the offer, but I must refuse. I have a duty to keep things secret," Misora replied. L had given her everything about the case anyone could have obtained—it did not seem likely she would be able to get any information from an inexperienced private detective. And of course, she had no intention of giving him anything. "I'm sure you have your secrets too."

"I don't."

"…Of course you do. You're a detective."

"Oh? Then I do."

Flexible.

Either way seemed to be fine with him.

"But it seems to me that solving this case must take precedence…

DEATH NOTE ANOTHER NOTE —

046

—

page.2 Ryuzaki

Very well, Misora. How about this: I will provide you with all the information I have in return for nothing."

"Eh…? Uh, I couldn't possibly…"

"Please. Ultimately, it does not matter if I solve the case or if you do. My client's wishes are to see the case solved, and only to see it solved. If you possess a sharper mind than my own, then telling you everything will be more effective."

All that sounded nice, but he could hardly be thinking that for real, so Misora's wariness of Ryuzaki grew even more pronounced. What was he after? A few minutes ago he had improvised a lie, claiming he thought she might be the killer returning to the scene of the crime, but that theory seemed to fit the man hiding under the bed far better than it did her.

"You may decide if you wish to give any of your information to me afterward. So, first, there's this," Ryuzaki said, pulling a folded piece of paper out of his jeans pocket. He held it out to her, without bothering to unfold it first. Misora took it, and unfolded it dubiously…it was a crossword puzzle. A grid, and clues in a tiny font. Misora had a hunch what this was.

"This is…"

"Oh? You knew about it?"

"Uh, no…not directly…" she stammered, unsure how to react. It seemed obvious that this was the same crossword that had been sent to the LAPD on July 22nd, but L had said the original puzzle had been thrown away, so was this a copy? How had this man…how had Ryuzaki been walking around with it jammed into his pocket? While she thought furiously, Ryuzaki stared at her appraisingly. As if he were evaluating her abilities based on her reaction…

"Allow me to explain. Last month, on the twenty-second of July, this crossword was sent to the LAPD by an unknown sender. Apparently, nobody could solve it, but if you were to solve this puzzle, it would give you the address of this house. Presumably it was a sort of warning from the killer to the police and to society in general. A declaration of war, one might say."

"I see. Still…"

Despite what L had said, part of her had still been dismissing the thing as just a crossword puzzle, but now that she could read the clues for herself, it did look extremely hard. The clues looked so frustrating that most people would give up before even trying to crack any of them. But the man across from her had solved it all by himself?

"You're sure the answer shows this address?"

"Yes. Feel free to keep it and solve it at your leisure if you doubt me. Either way, killers that send warnings are generally looking for attention, assuming they do not have some larger purpose. And the Wara Ningyo and locked room aspects of the case fit that profile. So it seems there is a very good chance of some other message…or something like a message, being left at the scene. Do you agree, Misora?"

"…"

Same conclusions as L.

Who was this man?

If he'd simply stated the same deductions as L, she could have dismissed them as extrapolated from the conversation he'd heard hiding under the bed, but for him to actually have a copy of the puzzle, a puzzle that only someone like L should have been able to acquire…The question of Ryuzaki's identity had become of critical importance to her once again.

"Excuse me," Ryuzaki said, putting both feet on the ground and heading, still stooped, for the kitchen—as if slipping out of the room to give Misora time to calm down. He opened the refrigerator with a practiced motion, as if this were his own house, stuck his arm inside, and took out a jar—and then shuffled back to the sofa, leaving the refrigerator door open. It appeared to be a jar of strawberry jam.

"What's with the jam?"

"Oh, this is mine. I brought it with me and put it there to keep it cold. It's time for lunch."

"Lunch?"

It did make sense that there would be no food in the refrigerator of a man who had died two weeks before, but lunch? Misora liked jam herself, but she didn't see any bread—and no sooner had the thought crossed her mind when Ryuzaki opened the lid, stuck his hand inside, scooped out some jam, and began licking it off his fingers.

"..."

Naomi Misora gaped at him.

Words failed her.

"...Mmm? Something the matter, Misora?"

"Y-you have strange eating habits."

"Do I? I don't think so."

Ryuzaki scooped another handful of jam into his mouth.

"When I start thinking, I get a craving for sweets. If I want to work well, jam is essential. Sugar is good for the brain."

"Hunh..."

Misora was of the opinion that his brain needed specialized medical attention more than sugar, but at that moment, she did not have the nerve to say so. His body language reminded her of Pooh Bear, but Ryuzaki was neither yellow nor adorable, and less a bear inclined to doing nothing than a rather tall man with a pronounced slouch. When he had eaten four handfuls of jam, he proceeded to put his lips directly on the rim of the jar like it was a cup of tea and slurp the contents noisily. Within moments he had consumed the entire jar.

"Sorry for the delay."

"Oh...not at all."

"I have more jam in the refrigerator if you'd like some?"

"N-no thanks…"

That meal was like torture. She would turn it down if she were starving to death. Every fiber of her body rejected Ryuzaki. Completely. Misora had never had much confidence in her ability to fake a smile, but the one she was aiming at him now was extremely convincing.

People can smile even when terrified.

"Okay," Ryuzaki said, licking jam off his fingers, giving no sign how he took her reaction. "So, Misora, let's go."

"Go? Go where?" Misora asked, desperately trying to figure out a way to refuse on the off chance that he should attempt to shake her hand.

"Obviously," Ryuzaki said. "To continue our investigation of the scene, Misora."

At this moment, Misora should still have been capable of (arbitrarily) choosing her path in what was to come. She could have physically thrown Ryuzaki out of Believe Bridesmaid's house, and we could even say that doing so would have been the most sensible reaction to his presence, but despite being very, very tempted to take the sensible approach, Misora made up her mind to let him stay. More than anything, the possibility that he had overheard her conversation with L rated Ryuzaki as a hazard, and even without that he was suspicious, sinister, and had a copy of the crossword puzzle, which clinched the deal. She needed to keep him under observation until she had a better idea who he was. Certainly, anyone who knew more about the situation, anyone like me, can tell that this was exactly what Ryuzaki was hoping for, exactly what he was trying to achieve, but it would be too much to ask to expect Naomi Misora to have realized this so soon. After all, several years after the Los Angeles BB Murder Cases, when she was killed by Kira, Misora remained convinced that she had never met L in person, that she had only obeyed his voice-augmented commands through her computer screen. Depending on how you look at it, this might have been a good thing for the world—even the murderer Kira, had he known just how deep Misora's connection with L was, would never have killed her so quickly. L's life was only extended by a few extra years, but even that may well be thanks to Misora...nah, not even worth speculating about.

Back to the point.

Anyone who has read Sherlock Holmes will remember the vivid descriptions of the great detective bounding around the room, peering closely at everything through a magnifying glass. An iconic image that is so firmly associated with the old detective novels that one never sees a detective behave like that anymore. For that matter, the term detective novel is almost never used—they get called mystery novels, or thrillers. Nobody wants a detective who actually deduces anything—much more exciting if they just blurt out the truth. The process of deduction requires such a lot of work—and no real genius ever needs to work. Same goes for boys' comics in Japan, popular all over the world. The most popular books all have heroes with exceptional powers.

So when they entered the bedroom and Ryuzaki abruptly went down on all fours, just like he had been when he emerged from under the bed, and began crawling all over the room (albeit without a magnifying glass) Misora was genuinely surprised. Being under the bed had not been the only reason for this posture, apparently. He seemed so accustomed to spending time on all fours that he looked ready to climb up the wall and across the ceiling.

"What are you waiting for, Misora? Join me!"

"!!"

Misora shook her head so quickly it blurred.

It was beneath her pride as a woman. No, as a human being—

joining him would forever part her from something extremely important.

"Oh? What a shame," Ryuzaki said, apparently never having possessed that critical something in the first place. He shook his head sadly and continued searching the room.

"B-but Ryuzaki...I don't think there's anything left here to find. I mean, the police already searched it pretty thoroughly..."

"But the police overlooked the crossword puzzle. It would not surprise me at all if they overlooked something else in here."

"If you put it that way...but there's just so little to work with. I wish I had a clue to what I was supposed to be looking for—the room's too empty to just rifle through it at random. And the house is too big."

"A clue...?" Ryuzaki said, pausing mid-crawl. Then he slowly bit his thumbnail—so carefully that it looked thoughtful, but the movement was so infantile that it made him look equally stupid. Misora could not decide which emerged victorious. "What do you think, Misora? When you came in, did you think of anything? Any idea that might help narrow it down?"

"Well...yeah, but..."

There had been one thing—the cuts on the victim's chest. She wasn't at all sure she should tell Ryuzaki about those. But it was also true that she was getting nowhere otherwise...either with the case, or with Ryuzaki. Possibly she should test him, just as he had observed her reaction when he handed her the crossword puzzle. If she played her cards right, she might figure out if he'd heard her phone call from under the bed.

"Right...Ryuzaki. As thanks for earlier, rather than a complete exchange of information...have a look at this photograph."

"Photograph?" Ryuzaki said, with a reaction so exaggerated one would think he had never before heard the word. He came over toward her...still on all fours, and without bothering to turn around.

He essentially reversed toward her, a spectacle that would surely have made a small child cry.

"A picture of the victim..." Misora said, handing him the autopsy photograph.

Ryuzaki took it, nodding gravely—or making a show of nodding gravely. So much for her test—from his outward reaction, she could read absolutely nothing.

"Well done, Misora!"

"Yes?"

"The news did not mention that the body was cut up like this, which means this photograph is from the police files. I'm impressed that you were able to get your hands on it. You're obviously no ordinary detective."

"...So how did you get hold of the crossword puzzle, Ryuzaki?"

"That would be my duty to keep secrets."

Her follow-up was knocked aside just as easily. She belatedly wished she had allowed him to deny that he had secrets, that she had never taught him the concept in the first place.

She was also pretty sure it didn't make sense grammatically.

"I will not ask how you obtained this photograph, either, Misora. But how does this relate to your idea?"

"Yes, well...I wondered if the message might be on something that isn't in the room anymore, but was in the room at the time. And the most obvious thing that should be here, but isn't..."

"Is the room's occupant, Believe Bridesmaid. Clever."

"And if you look at that picture from the right angle...do the wounds look like letters to you? I wondered if it might be some sort of message..."

"Oh?" Ryuzaki said, holding the picture perfectly still while moving his head around jerkily. Were there no solid bones in his neck? He moved like a contortionist. Misora fought the urge to look away. "No, not letters..."

"No? …I thought it was reading too much into it…"

"No, no, Misora, I am not denying the entire idea, just a portion of it. These are not letters, but Roman numerals."

"…"

Oh.

Right, Roman numerals, the same ones that she saw on clocks and whatnot every day—V and I, obviously, and C, M, D, X, and L…she should have figured it out when she saw three I's next to each other—it wasn't three I's, but III. But there had been an L right after them, and she had connected that with the detective's name and distracted herself.

"I is one, II is two, III is three, IV is four, V is five, VI is six, VII is seven, VIII is eight, IX is nine, X is ten, L is fifty, C is one hundred, D is five hundred, M is one thousand. So these wounds can be read as 16, 59, 1423, 159, 13, 7, 582, 724, 1001, 40, 51, and 31," Ryuzaki said, reading the complicated numbers without a second's pause. Was he good with Roman numerals, or was his mind really working that quickly? "It's just a photograph, so I might not be reading them correctly, but there's an eighty percent chance I'm right."

"Percent?"

"However, I'm afraid that doesn't change the situation. Unless we can figure out what those numbers are supposed to mean, it would be dangerous to assume they are a message from the killer. Perhaps they are simply misdirection."

"…Excuse me, Ryuzaki," Misora said, taking a step backward.

"For what?"

"I need to fix my makeup."

Without waiting for a response, Misora left the bedroom and climbed the stairs, heading for the second (not the first) story toilet. She locked the door from the inside and took out her cell phone. She hesitated for a moment, then called L. On the number five line. There was a brief beeping as it cleared a few scramblers, and then it finally connected.

"What is it, Naomi Misora?"

The synthetic voice.

L.

Lowering her voice and hiding her mouth behind her hand, Misora said, "Something I need to report."

"Progress in the case? Very fast work."

"No...well, a little. I may have stumbled across a message from the killer."

"Wonderful."

"But it wasn't me that figured it out. How can I put this...a kind of...mysterious private detective..."

A mysterious private detective.

The expression nearly made her laugh.

"...just showed up."

"I see," the synthetic voice said, and fell silent.

It was an uncomfortable silence for Misora—after all, she had made the decision to show Ryuzaki the picture and attempt to test him. When L said nothing, Misora proceeded to explain what Ryuzaki had said about the autopsy photograph. And that he had a copy of the crossword puzzle. This piece of information at last produced a reaction from L, but since it was a synthetic voice, she couldn't read the emotion behind it.

"What should I do? Frankly, I think it's dangerous to take my eyes off him."

"Was he cool?"

"Hunh?"

L's question came completely out of left field, and he was forced to ask it a second time before Misora answered, still unable to work out what he was driving at.

"No, absolutely not," she said, honestly. "Creepy and pathetic, and so suspicious that if I weren't on leave, I'd move to arrest him the moment I laid eyes on him. If we divided everyone in the world into those that would be better off dead and those that wouldn't, there's no doubt in my mind that he'd be the former. Such a complete freak that it amazes me he hasn't killed himself."

"…"

There was no answer.

What was this about?

"So, Naomi Misora, your instructions."

"Yes?"

"I imagine you are thinking much the same thing as I am, but let this private detective do what he likes for the moment. Partly because it is dangerous to let him out of your sight, but more importantly because it is important to observe his actions. I believe the credit for the autopsy photograph deductions belongs to you more than it does him, but he is clearly no ordinary person."

"I agree."

"Is he close by?"

"No, I'm alone. I'm calling from the bathroom, upstairs and to the back of the house, away from the bedroom."

"Go back to his side soon. I will follow up on him, and try to discover if a detective named Ryuzaki has actually been hired by Believe Bridesmaid's parents."

"Okay."

"You can use the same line the next time you call."

And he hung up.

Misora snapped her phone shut.

She needed to go back soon, so he would not be suspicious, but she had left his side with rather unnatural timing, she thought, leaving the bathroom.

Ryuzaki was standing just outside the door.

"Eek…!"

"Misora. You were up here?"

He was not on all fours, but even so, Misora gulped. How long had he been there?

"After you left the room, I discovered something interesting, and was unable to wait. So I came to get you. Are you quite finished?"

"Y-yes..."

"This way."

He trotted off, still hunched, toward the stairs. Still shaken, Misora followed him. Had he been listening through the door? This question tortured her. He discovered something interesting? That might just be a turn of phrase...she had kept her voice so low there was no way he could have heard her, but either way, he had almost certainly been trying to. Which meant...

"Oh, Misora..." Ryuzaki said, not turning around.

"Y-yes?"

"Why didn't I hear the toilet flush before you left the room?"

"...It's rather rude to ask a girl something like that, Ryuzaki," Misora managed, wincing slightly at her mistake. Ryuzaki did not appear to be phased.

"Is it? Nevertheless...if you forgot to flush, it is not too late. You can still go back. The genders are equal when it comes to sanitary behavior."

"..."

What a horrific way of putting it.

In every meaning of the word.

"I was on the phone. Just a regular check-in with my client. But I did not want to you hear some of it."

"Oh? But either way, from now on, I recommend flushing. It provides good camouflage."

"I suppose it does."

They reached the bedroom. Ryuzaki went down on all fours as he crossed the threshold. It looked less like an investigation method modeled on Sherlock Holmes than some sort of religious jinx.

"Over here."

Ryuzaki scrabbled across the carpet toward the bookshelves. Believe Bridesmaid's bookshelves, with their fifty-seven tightly packed books. It was the first place Misora had checked after talking with L.

"You said you found something new?"

"Yes. Something new—no, let us be bold. I have uncovered an important fact."

"…"

His attempt at sounding cool annoyed her.

She ignored it.

"So you found a clue of some kind on the bookshelf, you mean?"

"Look here," Ryuzaki said, pointing to the right side of the shelf second from the bottom. There was an eleven-volume set of a popular Japanese comic book named *Akazukin Chacha*.

"…What about it?"

"I love this manga."

"You do?"

"I do."

"…"

How was she supposed to respond? In direct contrast to her wishes, she felt her expression softening, but with no attempt to probe her inner struggle, Ryuzaki continued.

"You're nikkei, aren't you?"

"Nikkei…? My parents are both from Japan. My passport's American now, but I lived in Japan until after high school…"

"So you must know this manga. Min Ayahana-sensei's legendary creation. I read every issue as it was serialized. Shiine is so adorable! I liked the anime just as much as the manga. Love and courage and hope—Holy Up!"

"Ryuzaki, are you going to go on like this for a while? If so, I can wait in the other room..."

"Why would you do that when I'm talking to you?"

"Er, um...I mean, I liked *Akazukin Chacha* too. I watched the anime. I also experienced the love, courage, hope and Holy Up."

She longed to inform him exactly how little interest she had in his hobbies, but it was doubtful whether this private detective would be able to understand opinions directed at him from anywhere near common sense. As questionable as Ryuzaki himself.

Or was that overstating things?

"Good. We shall discuss the pleasures offered by the anime in detail on some other occasion, but for the moment, look here."

"Hunh..." Misora said, obediently looking at the volumes of *Akazukin Chacha* on the shelf.

"Notice anything?"

"Not really..."

It was just a bunch of comics. At most they could tell that Believe Bridesmaid was fluent in Japanese, and liked manga...but there were lots of people like that in America. Reading the original Japanese instead of a translated version was not terribly unusual, either. With the advent of Internet shopping, it had become extremely easy to obtain them.

Ryuzaki's dark-rimmed eyes were staring fixedly at her. Uncomfortable, Misora avoided his gaze, checking each volume individually. But even after she'd finished checking them out, she'd found no curious facts or anything like a clue.

"I don't see anything...something about one of these comics?"

"No."

"...Hunh?" There was more than a hint of anger in her voice.

She did not like being made fun of.

"No? What do you mean..."

"*Not one of these,*" Ryuzaki said. "Something that should be here, but isn't. Misora, you're the one who figured this out—any messages from the killer are indicated by the absence of what should be here. You're the one who figured out that this must refer to the body of Believe Bridesmaid. I didn't think I would need to explain this to you—look closely, Misora. They aren't all here. Volumes four and nine are missing."

"Eh?"

"*Akazukin Chacha* ran for thirteen volumes. Not eleven."

Misora looked down at the books again, and the numbers went from one, two, and three to five, six, seven, and eight to ten. If Ryuzaki was right, and there were thirteen volumes in all, then two volumes were missing—volumes four and nine.

"Hmm…right. But…Ryuzaki, so what? You mean the killer took those two volumes with him? It's certainly a possibility, but it seems equally likely they were missing in the first place. Maybe he planned to pick them up soon. Not everyone reads manga in order, you know. I mean, he seems to have stopped halfway through the *Dickwood* series, up here…"

"Impossible," Ryuzaki said, firmly. "No one on earth would ever skip two volumes in the middle of *Akazukin Chacha*. I am absolutely sure this fact would pass muster in court."

"…"

Had this man ever been in a court?

"Or at least, if the members of the jury knew much about Japanese comics."

"What a biased jury."

"The killer has obviously taken them with him," Ryuzaki said, blatantly ignoring her.

Misora wasn't about to let this pass. Her feet were firmly planted on more realistic ground.

"But you have no proof of that at all, Ryuzaki. It's equally possible he just loaned them to a friend."

"*Akazukin Chacha*?! You wouldn't even loan it to your parents!

You'd tell them to buy their own! The only possible explanation is that the killer took them away!" Ryuzaki insisted, quite forcefully.

He didn't stop there.

"Furthermore, no one on earth would ever want to read only volumes four and nine—I'd bet my jam on it!"

"If you're referring to the jam you were eating earlier, a jar of that only goes for around five bucks."

Min Ayahana-sensei would be disappointed.

"So it follows, Misora, that when the killer removed those two volumes from the room he had some other, completely unrelated reason for doing so."

"...Since it is true that those two volumes are missing, ignoring logic and possibility for the moment and following along with this hypothetical...it's still strange, isn't it? I mean, Ryuzaki, this bookshelf..."

Was packed full. So tightly that removing a book from it had been rather difficult. If he had really removed two volumes of manga, then there should be that much of a gap...or wait...

"Ryuzaki. Do you know how many pages there are in volumes four and nine of *Akazukin Chacha*?"

"I do. 192 pages and 184 pages."

"..."

She had not actually expected him to know the answer...but 192 plus 184 was 376 pages. Misora glanced along the shelf, looking over the fifty-seven books for a volume the same thickness as 376 pages of manga. It did not take long. There was only one book that thick on this shelf—*Insufficient Relaxation* by Permit Winter.

When she took it off the shelf it did, indeed, turn out to be exactly 376 pages.

"..."

Hopefully, Misora flipped through the pages, but she didn't see anything particularly interesting.

"What is it, Misora?"

"Oh...I was wondering if the killer had put a book on the shelf to replace the two he took off, and if that book was the real message..."

Assuming that it had really been Believe Bridesmaid who had carefully arranged his books to fill the shelf exactly. It might have been a much more haphazard affair, and the killer had arbitrarily filled it with books taken from another room—and by extension of that line of thought, there was no telling if *Akazukin Chacha* actually belonged to Believe Bridesmaid in the first place. With the lack of bookmarks, it might all be part of the killer's message—but so what if it was? If that was the case, it just made it all the more convincing that there was some sort of message here. But if there was nothing unusual about the books themselves, then the whole theory fell apart. It was nothing more than idle fancy.

"Not a bad idea. No, rather a good idea—nothing else makes sense," Ryuzaki said, reaching out toward Misora.

For a moment she thought he wanted to shake her hand, and panicked, but then she realized he just wanted *Insufficient Relaxation*. She handed it to him. Ryuzaki plucked it from her grasp with his index finger and thumb, and began reading. Speed reading—he went through all 376 pages remarkably quickly.

It took him less than five minutes to read the entire book.

Misora was tempted to make him read Natsuhiko Kyogoku.

"I see!"

"Eh? You found something?"

"No. There's absolutely nothing here. Don't look at me like that. I swear, I'm not joking. This is just an ordinary entertainment novel, not a message, or even a metaphor like the Wara Ningyo. And of course, there are no letters of any kind hidden between the pages, nor anything scribbled in the margins."

"The margins?"

"Yes, there was nothing in the margins but page numbers."

"'Page numbers'?" Misora echoed. Page numbers...numbers? Numbers, like...Roman numerals? "Ryuzaki, assuming those cuts on the victim's chest were Roman numerals, what did they say?"

"16, 59, 1423, 159, 13, 7, 582, 724, 1001, 40, 51, and 31."

Good memory. Didn't even need to see the picture again. Nearly a photographic memory—first the number of pages in the books, and now this.

"What about them?"

"I was just wondering if they were pointing at the pages in this book, but...two of the numbers were four digits. The book's only 376 pages long. They don't match."

"Yes...no, Misora, what if it wraps around? For example, 476 could be seen as 376 plus one hundred, and indicate page 100."

"...Meaning what?"

"I don't know. But let's try it out...16 is easy, page 16. 59, 1423, 159, 13, 7, 582, 724, 1001, 40, 51, 31..."

He narrowed his dark-rimmed eyes.

Not even looking at the book. Seriously? Even at the speed he was reading, he'd managed to memorize the entire contents perfectly? Was that even possible? Could he really do that? Either way, Misora could only stand and wait.

"...I see."

"That there's nothing there?"

"No...there is something there. Something very specific, Misora." Ryuzaki handed *Insufficient Relaxation* back to Misora. "Open it to page 16," he said.

"Okay."

"What is the first word on that page?"

"Quadratic."

"Next is page 59. The first word on that page?"

"Ukulele."

"Next is page 295. 1423 wraps around three times, and hits 295 on the fourth lap. First word is?"

"Tenacious."

They continued. 159 was page 159, 13 was page 13, 7 was page 7, 582 was page 206, 725 was page 348, 1001 was page 249, 40 was page 40, 51 was page 51, and 31 was page 31, and on each page, Misora read out the first word. In order: "rabble," "table," "egg," "arbiter," "equable," "thud," "effect," "elsewhere," and "name."

"So."

"So...what about it?"

"Take the first letter of each word."

"The first letter? Um..."

Misora went back through each page again. She did not have a bad memory, but was unable to remember twenty words at one go. At least, not without being warned in advance that she would be required to do so.

"Q-U-T-R-T-E-A-E-T-E-E-N...qutr tea teen? What?"

"Very similar to the second victim's name, don't you think?"

"I suppose..."

The second victim. The thirteen-year-old girl.

Quarter Queen.

"There is a vague resemblance...Quarter Queen...only four letters are different."

"Yes. However..." Ryuzaki said, reluctantly. "Four letters out of twelve is too many. One third of them are wrong. If even one letter is different, then the entire theory falls apart. Unless it matches perfectly, it's not worth calling a message. I thought there might be something there, but it may well be just a coincidence..."

"But...for a coincidence..."

It was so obvious.

How could it be?

It had to be intentional.

Intentional...or abnormal.

"Still, Misora...if it doesn't match, it doesn't match. We were very close, but..."

"No, Ryuzaki. Think about it. All four wrong numbers match up with numbers over 376. They're all numbers where we had to wrap around."

She flipped through the pages, checking them again. Page 295, first word: tenacious, first letter: T, second letter E, third letter N, fourth letter...A.

"Three times through, and on the fourth lap...we don't use the first letter, but the fourth letter. Not T, but A. And with 582, and 'arbiter,' once around and on the second lap gives us R instead of A. That turns Qutrtea into Quarter."

By the same logic, "equable" was 724, so one time through, on the second lap, the second letter: Q. And with 1001 and "thud"—not T, but U. That made Eteen into Queen. Quarter Queen.

L had been right.

The killer had left a message.

The cuts on the body, the two missing books—the killer had left a message. Just like the crossword puzzle he'd sent to the police, a message describing his next victim...

"Nice work, Misora," Ryuzaki said, unruffled. "Very good deduction. I would never have thought of it."

page.3
Opposition

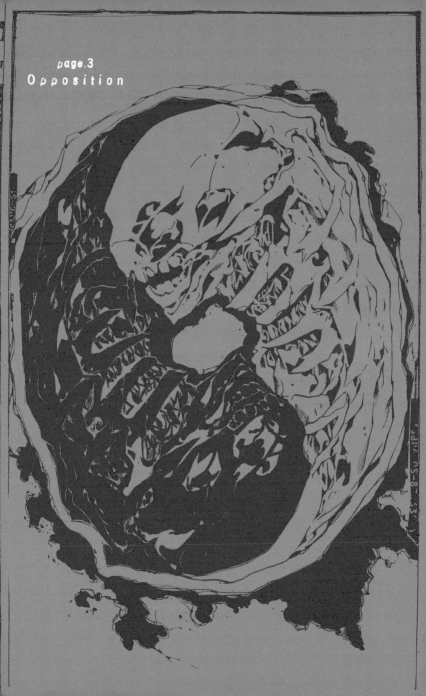

If we must discuss why L so adamantly refused to reveal himself, we can explain it very simply: doing so was dangerous. Very dangerous. While the world leaders should make efforts to ensure the safety of all the finest minds, not only for detectives, the fact is that the current societal systems do not allow for this, and L believed he had no choice but to protect his mind under his own power. By simple arithmetic, L's ability in 2002 was the equivalent of five ordinary investigative bureaus, and seven intelligence agencies (and by the time he faced off against Kira, those numbers had leapt upward several more notches). This is easy to think of as a reason to respect and admire someone, but let me say this as clearly as possible: that much ability in one human is extremely dangerous. Modern danger management techniques rely heavily on diffusing the risk, but his very existence was the exact opposite. In other words, if someone was planning to commit a crime, they could greatly increase their chances of getting away with it by simply killing L before they began. That was why L hid his identity. Not because he was shy, or because he never left the house. To ensure his own safety. For a detective of L's ability, self-preservation and the preservation of world peace were one and the same, and it would not be correct to describe his actions as cowardly or self-centered. While I don't personally relish the thought of comparing them, if Kira had had the ability to kill someone by writing their name in a notebook only, then he would hardly have publicized that fact for exactly the same reasons. The most intelligent people disguise the fact that they are intelligent. Wise men do not wear nametags. The more people talk about their own skills, the more desperate they are—their work should speak for itself.

So whenever L was working, he would usually have someone else as his public face—and in this particular case, the FBI agent Naomi Misora was filling that role. Misora understood this right from the very beginning. That she was L's shield. And just how much danger her direct link to L put her in...Misora tried many times to figure out Ryuzaki's true nature, but no matter how optimistically she viewed the situation, she was never able to view it as anything better than, "He *probably* didn't hear *much* of the conversation," and that supposition never felt very secure. If Ryuzaki had noticed the connection between Misora and L, and he leaked that information in the right places, then she would be in grave danger before you could say...before you could even think of saying anything, and the thought of that made even Misora nervous. And given Ryuzaki's obvious deductive abilities...a day after they had solved the message hidden in Believe Bridesmaid's bedroom, Misora had begun to wonder if her own deductions had not been guided by Ryuzaki's skillful lead. At the time, she had felt like it was all her doing. But thinking back on it, the page numbers, the laps around the book—she had only noticed it because Ryuzaki had laid the groundwork. Had there been any real reason for her to go through the book herself, reading out each word? She couldn't dismiss the idea that this had all been a performance to make Misora feel like she was taking part in solving the riddle, and that he had neatly allowed her to make the final breakthrough after carefully solving everything else for her. All this might be nothing but paranoia brought about by the pressure of having L backing her...but discovering the name of the second victim on Believe Bridesmaid's bookshelf was a big score for her investigation. She had checked afterward, and the second victim was the only person in the entire Greater Los Angeles area named Quarter Queen—but this came as no relief.

August 16th.

Naomi Misora was downtown, on Third Avenue, visiting the scene of the second murder. She did not know her way around the neighborhood, so she had to puzzle over a map to find her way here. Without knowing when a fourth murder would occur, part of her had wanted to come straight here from Believe Bridesmaid's, but she had other things to check up on first, so much evidence to sift through, and given the problem of transportation, she had ended up waiting till the next day. It was now three days since the third murder—nine days, four days, nine days, and if the killer planned to kill after four days again, then the next murder would happen tomorrow, but she had no other choice. No way to prevent it from happening. So she did the only thing she could do. Search for evidence that would allow her to take on the approaching crisis.

According to L's investigation, a detective named Rue Ryuzaki *had* actually been hired by Believe Bridesmaid's parents—and not only them, but relatives of the second victim, Quarter Queen, and the third victim, Backyard Bottomslash, had asked Ryuzaki to investigate the matter as well. This was a little too good to be true, in Misora's opinion, but if L said so, she had to accept it. There was no room for doubt. But even L had not yet managed to dig out anything about Ryuzaki's background, so she had been asked to keep watching, to cooperate with Ryuzaki and pretend they were investigating the matter together.

Had L really reached no conclusions about Ryuzaki at all? Misora spent a few minutes pondering this question. Perhaps explaining it to her would simply be too dangerous…Misora never thought for a moment that L was giving her all the information he had. Ryuzaki might fall into that category—but this might also be baseless paranoia. Ryuzaki was certainly suspicious, but he had not done anything overtly evil, so it didn't go past that.

The thought of seeing him crawl around the crime scene on all fours again today was undeniably depressing (she'd had nightmares about it. Misora normally took forever to wake up, but this particular dream sent her flying out of bed). And at that moment, on August 16th, at ten o'clock in the morning...

Naomi Misora was assaulted.

She was taking a shortcut through a deserted, dark alley when someone hit her from behind with a blackjack. Or, rather, failed to hit her—since she ducked in time, and avoided it. A blackjack is a light weapon—a very simple affair, consisting of nothing but a little bag filled with sand. Its simplicity made it very easy to conceal, and it was an undeniably effective weapon. She heard it slicing through the air as it brushed past her hair. Misora had been in danger since the moment she agreed to be L's hands, eyes, and shield, so she was not terribly surprised, and reacted quickly. It managed to drive all thoughts of Ryuzaki out of her mind instantly, which was fine by her. She hit the asphalt with both hands, pushing down to power her legs upward—twisting sideways upside down, sending her foot toward her assailant's chin. She missed. But no matter—the main goal of this movement had been to turn herself around and get a look at her assailant. There was only one, and he was wearing a mask. She was surprised at the lack of backup, but in addition to the blackjack, he was carrying a hefty club in his left hand, putting her at a distinct disadvantage. This was no ordinary thug. Like the day before, Misora did not have a gun. And, obviously, no badge or hand-cuffs. Running would have been the most logical choice, but Misora did not have the kind of retiring personality that would allow her to run when attacked. Her nickname in the FBI was Misora Massacre. Clearly, there was a certain degree of malice behind the name, but it was not entirely without cause. She bounded upward, landing with her legs apart, her right hand in front of her face and her center of gravity low, facing her assailant and swaying slightly, ready to fight. He hesitated for a moment when he saw her stance, but then swung at her—not the blackjack, but the club. Her upper body swayed, dodging it—and then she did a sort of cartwheel across the width of the narrow alley, aiming to slam her heel into her assailant's temple. He dodged again, but their fight was over. Misora had no intention of running, but her opponent did not seem to be as fiery. While Misora was getting to her feet, he spun around and ran away. Misora briefly considered chasing after him and took a couple of steps in that direction before abandoning the idea. She was pretty sure her assailant had been a man. She was pretty sure she could take him in a fight, but not in a footrace. She was not a strong runner. She didn't want to waste the energy.

She brushed her hair back into place, pulled out her cell phone, and called L. The phone rang, but nobody answered. The century's greatest detective was a busy man, and probably hard to reach outside of appointed times. Fortunately, she had not been injured, so the report could wait. Perhaps getting to the crime scene quickly was a better idea—being attacked like this had only increased Misora's suspicions concerning Ryuzaki. There was no way of telling if her assailant had been someone involved in the case, or someone who had nothing to do with it but knew about her connection to L, but either way, based on the timing of the attack, the odds of Ryuzaki being involved were not terribly low. Perhaps she should check into him herself, instead of leaving the investigation up to L…if only for self-preservation. She considered calling Raye, and having him check it out secretly, but first Misora left the alley behind.

As expected, Naomi Misora had not come after him.

He left the alley and jumped into the sedan that he'd left on the main road with the engine running. He turned a few corners quickly and checked the back mirror then parked in the lot he had picked out in advance. The sedan was a stolen car and would not lead back to him, so he had planned to abandon it here. One eye on the security cameras, he left the parking lot on foot, leaving the mask, blackjack, and club behind in the car. He had shoved them all under the seat. Leaving no fingerprints.

He had never planned to do anything to Naomi Misora today, not there. He had just been making a pass at her, to test her ability. He had attacked from behind, but not intended to hurt her—and certainly, he had no intention of killing her.

So there was no way she would die.

He had known she would dodge.

But even so, even with that in mind, that woman was impressive. Dodging his attack without even turning around, and moving instantly to an attack of her own—he could see why L was using her as his pawn. She had brains and guts—as she must.

She had the right.

She was worthy of being his opponent.

The assailant cracked his neck.

And with his head still hanging at an odd angle, he walked on down the street.

Misora's attacker…

The man behind the Los Angeles BB Murder Cases, Beyond Birthday, walked on down the street grinning cruelly.

"Ah, Misora. You're late," Ryuzaki said without turning around, the moment she entered apartment 605 where Quarter Queen had lived. "Please try to be on time. Time is money, and therefore life."

Sigh…

He was not down on all fours. She had come in just as he was inspecting the top shelf of a chest of drawers. But it was hard to think of this as nice timing. The drawer happened to be filled with the thirteen-year-old victim's underwear. Ryuzaki looked less like a detective investigating the scene than a pedophile stealing panties.

Not the best way to start the day. She'd been planning to funnel the frustration from her fight in the alley into a fairly aggressive approach to Ryuzaki, but he'd already yanked the rug out from under her. If it was deliberate, she would have been impressed, but that seemed unlikely. It seemed much more likely that Ryuzaki actually did have a fetish for children's underwear.

Misora sighed again, looking around the room—the entire apartment was smaller than Believe Bridesmaid's bedroom. The standard of living gap alone made it hard to see any connection between the first and second victims.

"We're talking a single mother here, right? Who has now moved back in with her parents? It must have been devastating…"

"Yes. These apartments were built for college students, intended to house only one, so a young girl and her mother living here attracted a fair amount of attention. I asked around a little this morning, and heard many interesting things. But most of them were already in the police report you showed me yesterday. The mother was out of town at the time of the murders, and the body was discovered by a college girl who lived next door. The mother first saw her daughter's body in the morgue."

"…"

As she listened to Ryuzaki speak, Misora checked the walls for the holes where the Wara Ningyo had been nailed. Of the four walls, the front wall—with the door in it—did not have a hole, but the other three did. Like in Believe Bridesmaid's bedroom, these holes indicated the location of the dolls.

"Something bothering you, Misora?"

"Yes…yesterday, *we*…" Misora said, emphasizing the plural, "…we decoded the message the killer left at the scene of the first murder, but…the Wara Ningyo and the locked room remain mysteries."

"Yes," Ryuzaki said, closing the door and dropping down onto all fours.

But unlike the first scene, two people had lived in this room, and there was quite a lot of furniture—the place was a mess. It looked rather difficult to crawl around in. Nevertheless, Ryuzaki persisted, and remained like that all the way to the other side of the room. Misora wished he would give up.

"But Misora, I don't think it's worth wasting much time on the locked room issue. This is not a mystery novel—realistically speaking, it's quite possible he simply used a spare key. There are no keys that can't be duplicated."

"True enough, but do you really think this killer would do something so prosaic? There was no real need to create a locked room in the first place. *But he did so anyway.* In which case, it might be a kind of puzzle…"

"Puzzle?"

"Or a game of some kind."

"Yes…yes, maybe…"

Misora looked back at the door she'd just come through. The design was different from the first murder scene (the difference between the front door of an apartment and the interior door of a house), but the construction and size were basically the same. A generic lock, simply made—very easy to break in when the house was empty by drilling through the door and turning the latch from the inside (known as a thumb turn lock) but obviously, there had been no holes in the door at any of the three scenes.

"What would you do, Ryuzaki? If you were trying to lock it from the outside?"

"Use a key."

"No, not like that…if you'd lost the key."

"Use a spare key."

"No, not like that…you don't have a spare key, either."

"Then I wouldn't lock it."

"…"

Not that he was wrong.

Misora reached out and shook the door.

"If this were a mystery novel…locked rooms are always created by a trick, like with a needle and thread, or…I mean, we call it a locked room, but these are just ordinary rooms, so they're never that secure. They aren't like Bridesmaid's bookshelves—they've got plenty of gaps and chinks around the frame. String could get under it easily…run a bit of string under the door, and tie it to the edge of the latch, and pull it…"

"Impossible. The gap isn't that big, and the angle would kill the force applied. You could try it out, but too much of the string would be pressed against the door. Before you could ever turn the latch, all the power you put into it would be eaten up pulling against the edge of the door. Pulling the door toward you."

"Yeah…but a lock this simple doesn't leave much room for a trick. The doors in detective novels usually have much more complicated ones."

"There are many ways to create a locked room. And we can't rule out the possibility that he had a key. More important, Misora, is the question of why the killer made a locked room. He had no need to make one, but he did so anyway. If he made a puzzle, why did he do it?"

"As a game. For fun."

"Why?"

"…"

You could ask that about any of this.

Why send a crossword puzzle to the LAPD, why leave a message on the bookshelf…and most of all, why kill three people? If the killer had a clear motive, then what was it? Even if the killings were random, something must have caused it…L had said so. But they still had no idea what linked the victims together.

Misora leaned against the wall and took some photographs out of her bag.

Pictures of the second victim, killed in this room—a young blonde girl, wearing glasses, lying on her face. Looking closely, her head had been dented in the shape of the weapon, and both her eyes had been poked out. The eyes had been crushed after death—like the cuts on Believe Bridesmaid's chest, this was mutilation of the corpse, with no relation to the cause of death. She had no idea what the killer had used to destroy the eyes, but trying to imagine the mental state of someone who could poke the eyes out of a cute little girl made Misora feel a little sick. Misora might be an FBI agent, but she was not prone to fits of righteousness—but there were some things that were simply unforgivable. What the killer had done to this second victim clearly fell into that category.

"Killing a child...how horrible."

"Killing an adult is also horrible, Misora. Killing children or adults—equally horrible," Ryuzaki said, unaffected, almost indifferent.

"Ryuzaki..."

"I've checked everything once," Ryuzaki said, standing up. He rubbed his hands on his jeans. Apparently he was at least aware that crawling around on the floor would make his hands dirty. "But I didn't find any money."

"...You were looking for money?"

Like a thief.

An extremely blatant one.

"No, just in case. One possibility is that the killer was after money, but in that case, the second victim is significantly more impoverished than the first and third victims. There was a chance they were hiding something, but apparently not. Let us take a break. Would you care for some coffee, Misora?"

"Oh...sure."

"One moment," Ryuzaki said, heading for the kitchen. Misora wondered if he had jam in the fridge again but decided that she didn't care. She abandoned that line of thought, and sat down at the table. She had somehow missed her timing to tell Ryuzaki about being attacked. Oh well. She might as well avoid mentioning it, and see how he reacted. She had no proof her assailant had anything to do with Ryuzaki, but not telling him made it easier for her to catch him off guard.

"Here you are."

Ryuzaki came back from the kitchen, carrying a tray with two cups of coffee on it. He placed one in front of Misora and the other opposite her, then pulled out the chair and assumed the strange sitting position he had demonstrated the day before, with his knees pulled up against his chest. Ignoring the matter of manners, it looked extremely difficult to sit like that—or was it? Misora wondered, and took a sip of coffee.

"Augh!" she yelled, spitting it out. "*Cough...hack...*urrghhh..."

"Something wrong, Misora?" Ryuzaki asked, innocently sipping his cup. "Once something has entered your mouth, it should never be spit out like that. And those terrible moans do nothing for your image, either. You are quite beautiful, so you should try to present yourself accordingly."

"M-murderously sweet...poisonous!"

"Not poison. Sugar."

"..."

So you're the killer?

Misora looked down at the contents of her cup...which was less a liquid than a paste. Less like sugar dissolved in coffee than sugar moistened with coffee—a gooey, gelatinous mass glistening majestically in her cup. While her attention had been distracted by Ryuzaki's posture, she had allowed this substance to touch her lips...

"I feel like I drank dirt."

"But dirt is not this sweet."

"*Sweet Dirt…*"

That sounded like an avant-garde piece. The diabolic gritty feeling in her mouth would not go away. Across from her, Ryuzaki was happily sipping away…lapping away. Apparently he had not made Misora's cup this way out of sheer spite, but this was, in his view, a perfectly normal amount of sugar.

"Whew…coffee always picks me up," Ryuzaki said, finishing his cup and what must have been at least two hundred grams of pure sugar. "Now then, to business."

Misora would have liked to get up and go wash the sugar out of her mouth, but she tried to ignore the impulse. "Go ahead," she said.

"About the missing link."

"Have you figured something out?"

"It seems the killer was definitely not after money…but last night, after I left your company, I noticed something interesting. A connection between the victims that nobody seems to have picked up on."

"What?"

"Their initials, Misora. All three victims have rather unique initials. Believe Bridesmaid, Quarter Queen, Backyard Bottomslash. B.B., Q.Q., B.B. Both their first and last names begin with the same letter…what is it, Misora?"

"Nothing…"

Was that all? Her disappointment had clearly shown on her face and interrupted Ryuzaki's line of thought, but she couldn't even be bothered to try and cover. What a pointless waste of time. Misora had noticed that the moment she first saw the victim's names. It wasn't worth bringing up like this.

"Ryuzaki…do you know how many people there are with alliterative initials in the world? In Los Angeles? There's only twenty-six letters in the alphabet, which means by a very rough calculation about one in twenty-six people has a name like that. Not even worth calling a connection."

"Oh? And I thought I was on to something…" Ryuzaki said, dejected. It was hard to tell how much of his reaction was genuine.

He appeared to be sulking, a trait which, in him, was not at all cute.

An absolutely terrible way to present oneself.

"I mean, you yourself are Rue Ryuzaki—R. R."

"Oh! I hadn't noticed."

"This is pointless."

She should never have expected anything from him. All that nonsense about him leading her through the deductions yesterday had been nothing but paranoia.

R.R.?

"Misora."

"Eh? Oh, what?"

"Since my deductions have come to naught, do you have any good ideas?"

"No, not really. I'm in the same boat as you…can't think of any real course of action except looking for another message, like we did yesterday. I feel like I'm dancing on the killer's palms, which irritates the hell out of me, but…"

"Then let us dance. Playing your enemy's game until he relaxes and lets a hint drop is a perfectly good strategy. So, Misora, if there is a message here…then where?"

"Well, we can at least guess the contents. Presumably the message has the third victim's name, Backyard Bottomslash, or her address. The crossword puzzle led to the first case, the book pages led to the second case, so…"

"Yes, I agree."

"But where that message is hidden, I have no idea. If we can figure out some sort of pattern, that would help us catch him, but…"

Something that *should* be here, but *wasn't.*

Ryuzaki had described it that way.

Referring to the victim, and to the bookshelves.

Was there something like that here? Something that should be here, but wasn't? Something that should be here but isn't here was starting to sound like a linguistic Möbius strip.

"So," Ryuzaki said. "If whatever we find will simply point us to the third victim, then perhaps it would be more effective if we skipped this scene and went right to the third one. After all, our goal is to prevent the fourth murder as well as solve the case."

"Yeah."

She was the one who had pointed out the chances of a fourth murder...but Ryuzaki's reaction had suggested he had been well aware of this possibility, which was why she hesitated now.

"The third murder has already happened, and we can't prevent that, but there is a chance that we can stop the fourth. Rather than waste time looking for a message when we already know what it says, it would be far more constructive to look for a message leading us to the fourth victim."

"But that just feels so submissive...like we're following his lead. I mean we might miss an important clue to his identity if we skip this room. Even if there isn't some clear evidence, we might get a feeling or a hunch that will help us out later. I agree that preventing the fourth murder is important, but if we focus on that too much, we'll lose the chance to get aggressive, to take control of the situation."

"Don't worry. I'm a top."

"A top?"

"An aggressive top," Ryuzaki said. "I have never once been submissive. One of the few things I can boast about. I have never even been submissive to a traffic signal."

"You really should."

"Never."

Adamant.

"Preventing the fourth murder should lead us directly to identifying and arresting the killer. This is what my clients want, more than anything. But I see your point as well, Misora. I'm already finished checking the room over, so while you are doing that, I would like to think about the third murder. Do you mind if I look at the file you showed me yesterday once more?"

"Work different angles? Fine by me…"

She'd never intended to cooperate with him anyway.

She took a binder out of her bag, checked to make sure it contained the file on the third murder, and handed it across the table to Ryuzaki.

"And…these are the crime scene photographs…"

"Thanks."

"But like I said, there haven't been any breakthroughs. The contents are the same as yesterday."

"Yes, I know. But there were a few things I wanted to double check…but this is a horrible picture, isn't it?" Ryuzaki said, putting one of the photographs down on the table where Misora could see it. It was a picture of Backyard Bottomslash's body. Misora had witnessed many horrible things during her career at the FBI, but this picture was so grotesque it gave her chills every time she saw it. Compared with this picture, cuts on a chest or crushed eyeballs were nothing.

The body was lying on its back, and the left arm and right leg had been chopped off at the root.

There was blood everywhere, all over the crime scene.

"They found the right leg abandoned in the bathroom, but they still have no idea where the left arm is…obviously, the killer took it with him. But why?"

"That question again? But Ryuzaki, isn't that another example of something that should be there, but isn't? In this case, the victim's

DEATH NOTE ANOTHER NOTE

083

THE LOS ANGELES BB MURDER CASES

left arm."

"The killer needed to cut off the left arm...but he did not bring the right leg with him. He just tossed it into the bathroom. What does that mean?"

"Either way, we're going over there this afternoon...but I'd like to spend a few hours here first."

"That sounds fine. Oh, yeah, there was a photo album belonging to the victim in that cabinet, Misora. Probably worth checking out. You might be able to find something about the victim's personality, or her friends..."

"Okay. I'll do that."

Ryuzaki turned his attention back to the file, and Misora stood up and made a beeline for the bathroom sink. She could no longer bear the grainy feeling in her mouth. She quickly gargled, but once was hardly enough, so she repeated the action two or three times.

She considered trying to contact L again. There had been no answer earlier, so...no, yesterday had been a house, but in a tiny apartment like this there was no getting away from Ryuzaki. Even if she called from the bathroom, he wouldn't even need to move over to the door to hear her. She would have to tell L about the attack eventually...or was that not something L would care about?

Misora looked up and saw her face in the mirror.

Naomi Misora.

This was her.

That much was clear.

Everyone knows the sensation of staring at a word for a long period of time until you start to wonder if it is really spelled correctly. In the same way, it was possible to doubt oneself, to wonder how long one could really be oneself. Was she still herself?

Which is why this was so important.

Why she stared at her reflection, confirming it again.

"But does L do the same?" she wondered suddenly. The century's greatest detective, someone who never showed himself in public, his identity unknown. How many people could say for sure that L was L? Was there anyone at all? Naomi Misora had no way of knowing, but she wondered if L, looking in a mirror, would even know who it was looking back at him.

"A mirror…a mirror?"

Hmm.

She almost had something there.

A mirror…right and left reversed in the reflection…reflected light…light reflecting off a smooth surface…glass, silver nitrate aqueous solution…silver? No, the material didn't matter, it was the quality that was important…that quality…the reflection of light…no, the reversal of right and left…in opposition?

"Opposition…the opposite…reversed!"

Misora bolted out of the bathroom, back to the table. Ryuzaki looked up from the file in surprise, his black-rimmed eyes opening wide.

"What's wrong?" he asked.

"The picture!"

"Hunh?"

"The photograph!"

"…Oh, you mean from the third crime scene?" Ryuzaki asked, placing the photograph on the table once more. The corpse, with the left arm and right leg severed. Misora pulled two other photographs out of her bag and placed them next to it. Crime scene photos of the first and second victims. Pictures of all the victims, showing the condition in which they were found.

"Notice anything, Ryuzaki?"

"What?"

"Anything about these photographs strike you as unnatural?"

"…They're all dead?"

"Being dead is not unnatural."

"How philosophic."

"Be serious. Look—the bodies are in different positions. Believe Bridesmaid is on his back, Quarter Queen is on her front, and Backyard Bottomslash is on her back. Back, front, back."

"…And you see a pattern in this? Connecting it to the nine days, four days, nine days between the murders? Meaning that tomorrow the fourth victim will be found lying on her front?"

"No, not at all. I mean, that might be true, but…I was thinking of a different possibility. In other words, *the very fact that Quarter Queen's corpse was left lying on her front is itself unnatural.*"

"…"

Ryuzaki's reaction was not very satisfactory—at least, it didn't look that way. Perhaps what Misora was trying to say wasn't getting across. She'd only just hit upon the idea and was talking quickly, fueled by excitement, without fully thinking it through, so that was understandable. "Let me think a minute," Misora said, sitting down in the chair next to him.

"Misora, when thinking, I recommend this posture."

"…'this posture'?"

With your knees against your chest like that?

He was recommending *that*?

"Seriously. It raises deductive ability by forty percent. You must try it."

"No, I…um…well, okay."

It wasn't like he wanted her to crawl, and it couldn't hurt to try. It might help her calm down a little from the high of inspiration.

She assumed the posture.

"…"

She regretted it a lot.

Even sadder was the fact that her ideas fell into place.

"Well, Misora? You mean Quarter Queen being on her front is a message from the killer? Pointing to the third victim…"

"No, not a message—this is the missing link, Ryuzaki. An extension of what you said about their initials..."

Two weird people sitting weirdly explaining weird bits of deduction was, Misora worried, a scene of overwhelming weirdosity. Nevertheless, she pointed to each of the pictures in turn, feeling that she had long since missed her chance to put her feet back on the floor. And this posture was a great deal easier to maintain than it looked.

"The victims' initials—B.B., Q.Q., B.B. Having both initials be the same isn't enough to be a missing link, but...both the first and the third victim have the same initials—B.B. If the second victim's initials were B.B. instead of Q.Q., then that would be a missing link, right?"

By simple arithmetic, twenty-six times twenty-six equals one in 676 people. Moving from matching initials to only one letter narrowed the odds by that much...and given how rare names beginning with B were, the actual number was even lower.

"An interesting theory. But Misora, the second victim's name is Quarter Queen, and her initials are Q.Q. Are you implying that perhaps she was killed by mistake? That the killer was aiming for someone with the initials B.B. and accidentally killed a Q.Q. instead?"

"What are you talking about? The message at the first scene clearly said Quarter Queen. There's no mistake there."

"Oh, right. I forgot."

"..."

Had he really forgotten? The phrase seemed phony...but if she puzzled out every one of Ryuzaki's reactions, they'd never get anywhere.

"Nine days, four days, nine days. B.B., Q.Q., B.B. Back, front, back. It's certainly possible to see this as alternating, like you suggested, and I certainly considered the idea, but...the killer's exacting approach to things makes that seem unlikely. Doesn't suit his personality. People that anal usually behave more coherently…"

"But the murder methods—strangulation, blunt force trauma, stabbing…they don't show any kind of consistency."

"Except that they're consistently different. He's painstakingly trying something new every time. But alternating is different from varied. Which is why, Ryuzaki, when I was looking in the mirror a moment ago, it hit me—B and Q are shaped the same."

"B and Q? They're completely different!"

"As capital letters. But what about lower case?" Misora said, drawing the letters on the table top with her fingertip. b and q. Over and over. b and q. b and q. b and q.

"See? Exactly the same shape! Just the other way around!"

"So that's why she's face down?"

"Exactly," Naomi Misora nodded. "A rough estimate of one in 676 people have the initials B.B., so if we take that as the missing link, then the killer must have had a lot of trouble finding victims. One was easy enough, but two, three, even four…even more so. He had no choice but to use a Q.Q. instead."

"I agree with everything except that last sentence. I don't believe it would be easier to find someone with the initials Q.Q. than it would be to find someone else with B.B. Even if it was, I think it's better to view the replacement as part of a puzzle designed for the investigation team. If they were all B.B. right from the start, the missing link would have been too obvious. But this is only supposition. No more than a thirty percent possibility."

"Thirty percent…"

Annoyingly low.

If this were a test, she'd have failed.

"Why?"

"According to your theory, your conclusion is that all of that tells us why Quarter Queen was found lying face down. Face down led you to reverse theory and to b and q…but this progression doesn't work logically, Misora."

"Why not?"

"Lower case," Ryuzaki said. "Initials are always capital letters."

"Oh…"

Right.

Initials were never written lower case. They were upper case every time. Quarter Queen was always Q.Q., never q.q. Just as B.B. was never b.b.

"And I thought I was on to something," Misora said, burying her face in her knees.

So close…but even the assertion that a killer this anal would never alternate had been more than a little bit of a stretch. But even so, the connection between b and q seemed so meaningful…

"Come now, Misora. Don't be so disappointed."

Sigh…

"Frankly, I'm glad your theory was wrong. If Quarter Queen had been killed as a substitute…that's a horrible reason for a child in her teens to die."

"Yeah…if you put it that way…"

Mmm? Misora frowned, suddenly. A moment before, Ryuzaki has insisted there was no difference between killing a child and killing an adult, but the motive for it bothered him? A reason like this one…did that have anything to do with anything? A child in her teens…

A child?

A child?

A little child?

"…No, Ryuzaki."

"Yes?"

"*In this case*—lower case is perfect," Misora said, her voice shaking.

Shaking with anger.

"That's why the killer chose a child."

A thirteen-year-old child.

Her initials.

Upper case, lower case.

"Because she was a child—lower case. And that's why she was face down—upside down!"

It would be some time later before Naomi Misora realized that it was Ryuzaki who had enthusiastically pointed out the matching initials, who had pointed out that the victim was a child, and who had given her the sugary coffee that had sent her into the bathroom, where the mirror provided the inspiration she needed to figure things out.

But either way...the Los Angeles BB Murder Cases.

The missing link had been found, the critical detail that would, in later years, give the case its name.

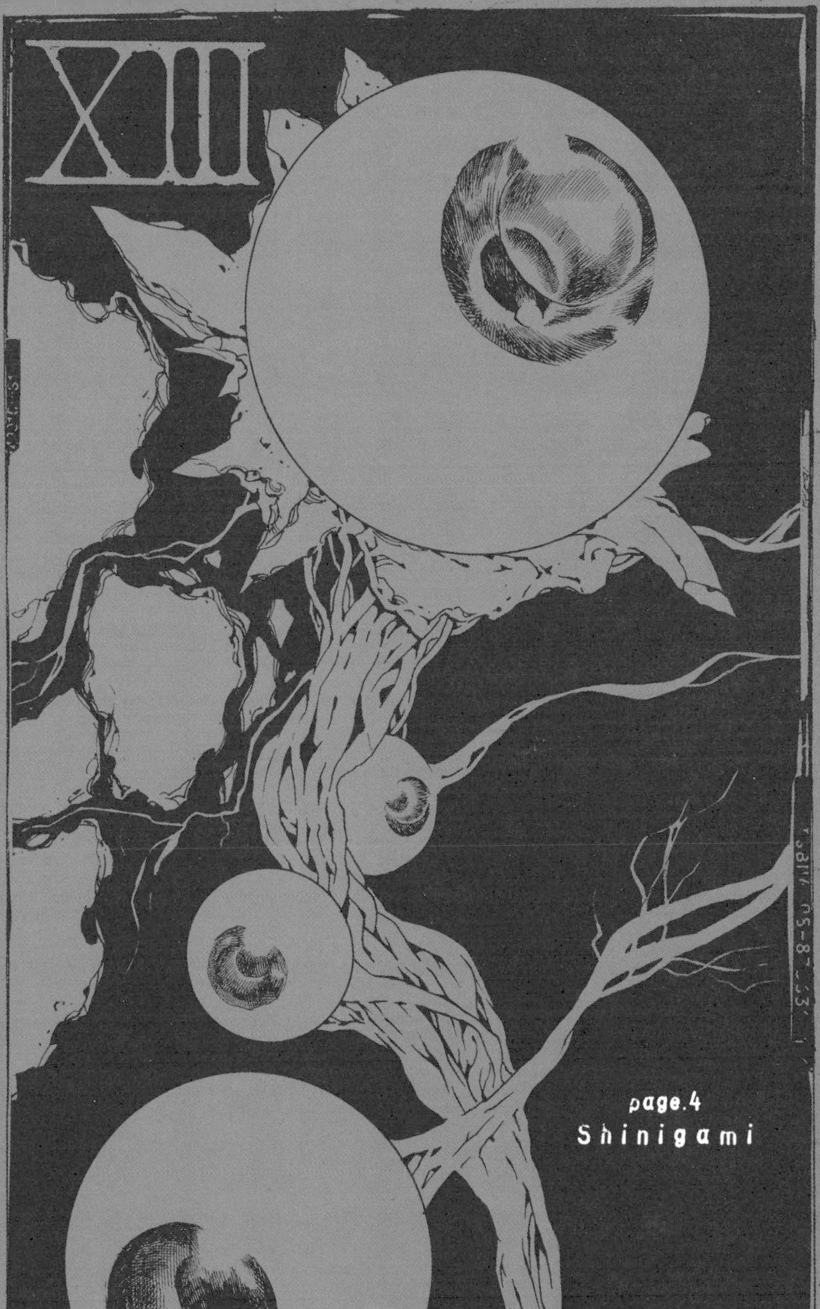
XIII
page.4
Shinigami

Imagine that you were going to kill someone. What do you think would be the most difficult part? Three, two, one…time's up! The correct answer: killing someone. Now, now, calm down—I swear I'm not making fun of you, or playing linguistic tricks here. I'm completely serious. People, in other words, humans, have not been designed to die that easily—at the least, people almost never grunt or moan and immediately fall over dead. Strangulation, blunt force trauma, stabbing—none of these kill people easily. Humans are surprisingly sturdy creatures. Additionally, people have a tendency to resist being killed. Nobody wants to be killed, and there's a good chance they'll try to kill you back. Physical strength in humans doesn't vary that much, and in a one-on-one fight, winning can be rather difficult. From this point of view, the ability to kill someone just by writing their name in a notebook is a flagrant violation of fair play, as I'm sure you can imagine.

However.

When Beyond Birthday went about committing this series of murders, he did not have any difficulty killing his victims. After all, the murders themselves were not his purpose, and he had no intention of expending undue effort on them—but even so, it was not easy to see exactly how he had avoided trouble. Certainly, he was using weapons and drugging his victims, but at this point all three of his victims had been killed without showing any real sign of resistance. In most cases, defense wounds are a key element in identifying the killer, but in this case the victims had all died as if it were only natural for them to have done so. The FBI Agent Naomi Misora never did understand why, and even the century's greatest detective, L, did not manage to create a working theory until several years after the case had ended.

But enough buildup.

Let me explain.

Beyond Birthday had the eyes of a shinigami congenitally. It was not particularly difficult for him to track down people with the initials B.B. or to find people who were fated to die on a certain day at a certain time. After all, there are over twenty million people in Los Angeles.

Killing people was, for him, normal.

Killing people who were fated to die anyway was no effort at all.

Mmm, I guess I should explain the idea of the eyes of a shinigami. The phrase is only too familiar to me, but if I don't explain it, some of you will cry foul. The eyes of a shinigami. These eyes could be given out by any shinigami in return for half the recipient's remaining life. They allowed the recipient to see people's names and remaining life. Normally contact with a shinigami was a prerequisite for acquisition, but Beyond Birthday had traded nothing—he had seen the world through those eyes since before he could remember.

He knew your name before you said it.

He knew the time of death of every person he met.

…I hardly need to explain just what effect this would have on his personality. You might think they would hardly be useful without a Death Note, but that is simply not the case. The ability to see someone's remaining life is the ability to see death. Death, death, death. Beyond Birthday lived his life unceasingly reminded that all humans would eventually die. From the time he was born he knew the day his father would be attacked by a thug and die, knew the day his mother would die in a train crash. He had these eyes before he was born, which is why he called himself Beyond Birthday. Which is why a child as strange as he was taken in by our home, sweet home—Wammy's House.

He was B.

The second child in Wammy's House.

"If only I could see the death of the world," Beyond Birthday murmured, on August 19th at 6 a.m., just as he woke up. He was lying on a simple bed on the second floor of a prefabricated storehouse borrowed under the name of a dormant company, in the suburbs of the west side of town. One of many hidden lairs located across the country, around the world. Why West L.A.? Because on that day, Naomi Misora, the suspended FBI agent fronting for the century's greatest detective, L, was going to be there.

"Naomi Misora. Naomi Misora. L's hands. L's eyes. L's shield. Ah ha ha ha ha ha ha ha! No, that's not right...I should laugh more like this...Kya ha ha ha ha ha ha ha! Yeah, that's better."

Kya ha ha ha ha ha ha ha ha ha.

Kya ha ha ha ha ha ha ha ha ha.

Laughing wildly, Beyond Birthday got out of bed. A harsh, cruel laugh, but an unnatural laugh, a phony laugh. As if laughing was just another task he had to perform.

Beyond Birthday remembered how he had attacked Naomi Misora three days before, on August 16th, in the alley downtown.

Of course, he had known when she would die—had seen how much life remained. Naomi Misora's life. It was not that time, on August 16th, but much, much later.

Which meant...

If he attacked her with intent to kill, he would absolutely fail. He knew that he would. Ensuring his path of escape was far more critical. Naomi Misora was nothing but L's servant, and if she died there would be dozens of replacements—from the FBI, the CIA, and the NSA—even the Secret Service. So he had only been testing her. Seeing if Naomi Misora was capable of being L's substitute.

"Hmmm...mmmm...hmmm...Huh huh huh huh...no, hee hee hee? I could go with ho ho ho ho, but that's a little too jolly...anyway. Oh, Naomi Misora—you are pretty good. A shame to waste someone like you in the FBI."

She had passed the test, so far.

Today she would visit the scene of the third murder, and she would most likely find the message Beyond Birthday had left for her. Then she would try to prevent the fourth murder, the victim Beyond Birthday had selected.

That was good.

Only then would the competition begin.

Only then would the real game start.

"...L."

The competition between L and B.

L and B's puzzle.

"If L's a genius then B's an extreme genius. If L's a freak, then B's an extreme freak. Now it's time to get ready. There are things I must do before B can surpass L. Henh henh henh henh."

This thought was the only thing that made him laugh without needing to think about it. And those that know will recognize the laugh of the shinigami.

Still grinning to himself, he faced the mirror, brushed his hair, and began applying his makeup. The reflection of himself in the mirror. Himself. As always, he could not see his own time of death. No more than he could see the death of the world.

So, August 19th.

Naomi Misora was in the west side of the city, in the townhouse where the third victim, Backyard Bottomslash, had lived. She had shared the place with a good friend of hers, but she had been killed while her friend had been out of town on business. Like the second

page 4 Shinigami

victim's mother, the roommate had moved back in with her parents after the murder.

Backyard Bottomslash's bedroom was on the second floor. There was a thumb turn latch just below the knob. And two holes on the walls where the Wara Ningyo had been. One on the far wall, directly opposite the door, and the other on the left hand wall. The floor was covered in a frankly bizarre number of stuffed animals for a twenty-eight-year-old, and the entire room was ornately decorated. There were stuffed animals piled against each wall. In order: two, five, nine, and twelve. Twenty-eight in all. While the room had been cleaned, it still smelled faintly of blood, which destroyed the effect of the decor.

"Where is Ryuzaki?"

She glanced down at the silver wristwatch on her left hand, and saw that it was already two thirty in the afternoon.

They were supposed to meet at two.

Misora had been here since early that morning, checking the place out in advance. She had searched the entire house, not just this room, but five hours later she had completely run out of things to do and was rather bored. And she had failed to uncover anything of interest, which had left her feeling frustrated. She bit her lip, annoyed that she had been unable to figure anything out without Ryuzaki around.

Then the phone in her bag rang. She answered quickly, assuming it was L, but it was her boyfriend and coworker, Raye Penber.

"Hello? Raye?"

"Yeah...let me speak quickly, Misora," Raye said, in a low voice. At this time of day there must be other people around him. "I checked up on what you asked me."

"Oh, thanks."

She'd asked him on the 16th, and it was now the 19th, and he was a very busy FBI agent, so this was pretty fast work. When she thought about how much he did for her, she found herself wanting to thank him every time she spoke to him.

"So?"

"Basically? There is no private detective named Rue Ryuzaki."

"So he's unlicensed?"

An unprivate detective.

He had said so himself.

"No. There are no records of anyone named Rue Ryuzaki at all. Not just in America, but in the records of every country in the world. The name Ryuzaki is reasonably common in your home country, but none of them are named Rue."

"Oh. He speaks Japanese like a native, so I thought he might be from there...so it's a fake name?"

"Presumably." Raye was silent for a moment, but then blurted, "Naomi! What are you doing?"

"You promised not to ask."

"I know I did. But your leave of absence will be over next week, and I was just thinking about the future...are you coming back to the FBI?"

"I haven't thought about it yet."

"I know I always say this, but..."

"Don't. I know what you're going to say, so don't say it."

"..."

"I don't have time. I'll call again."

Misora hung up without giving him a chance to respond. She spun the phone around between her fingers, feeling a little guilty. It wasn't that she hadn't thought about going back, but that she didn't want to think about it.

"Next week already? Nah...focus on the case at hand."

This might be running away, but since Ryuzaki still wasn't here... (She'd suspected the name was fake from the moment she met him, so she didn't particularly care...although she did wonder why he'd chosen that name in particular. But the real problem was why the victim's parents had hired a private detective that didn't exist)... Misora told herself to forget about it and go over the facts they had uncovered one more time.

First, the message left by the killer downtown, at the second crime scene. Naomi Misora had figured it out about an hour after they had found the missing link, that the victims were all connected by their initials. It was the eyeglasses the victim, Quarter Queen, was wearing. While she never got down on all fours the way Ryuzaki did, Misora had checked the room over from every conceivable angle, until her eyes ached from looking—without finding anything. Then she wondered if there was something on the victim's body, like the cuts on Believe Bridesmaid's chest, and had looked at the photos of the body again, but there was nothing there by the little girl lying face down, with her eyes crushed in...

When Misora was at her wit's end, Ryuzaki had said, "Maybe the damage to the eyes is a message." It sounded reasonable...in fact it seemed like the only possibility. Which meant...her eyes?

Misora had gone back to the cabinet and taken out the album of photographs again. She looked through them once more, checking every picture of the little blonde girl.

And realized...

...that there was not one picture of her wearing glasses.

The only picture of her with glasses was the one of her dead. Not because there wasn't a problem with her eyes—her chart was in the file, showing her right eye at 0.1 and her left at 0.05—but that she almost always wore contact lenses. After her death, the killer had put the glasses on and taken the contact lenses away. They were disposable lenses, so the investigative team had not noticed them missing. Misora had contacted the victim's mother, who had confirmed not only that Quarter Queen almost never wore glasses, not even at home, but that the glasses she was wearing in the crime scene photograph did not belong to her.

"Surprisingly hard to notice...who would ever think to ask if the glasses a murder victim was found wearing belonged to them? Literally a blind spot...perhaps that's what the crushed eyes mean?" Ryuzaki had said. "And the glasses looked so natural on her...making it even less likely that the police would notice. She never realized that she was *meant* to wear them."

"Um, Ryuzaki...that's getting a bit facetious."

"I was joking."

"That's what being facetious means."

"Then I was serious."

"Still facetious."

"Then I was deadly serious. Look! Don't you think she looks better?"

"W-well...I suppose..."

Facetious.

The mother had first seen her daughter's body in the morgue, and the glasses had already been removed. Which was probably all according to the killer's plan...by this point in time, what else could they think?

"The third murder happened in West L.A., near Glass Station— glasses. Very literal. But this doesn't give us the address, only the neighborhood..."

"No, if you narrow it down that much, then you can probably narrow it down all the way, Misora. All you have to do is look for someone in the area with the initials B.B., and you can fix on the address. In other words, the killer has assumed that by the time the second murder occurs, we would have figured out the missing link."

"Eh? But...we were only able to figure out that Q was actually B because the third murder had already taken place. At the time of the second murder, how could anyone have worked that out?"

"You don't need to. I mean, even at the third murder, there's no real way to tell if B is the main letter and Q the reverse, or the other way around. The fourth murder could be another child with the initials Q.Q. and flip the idea. It's possible he's mainly killing children, and is really after Qs. From our current data, we have no idea why he's aiming for B.B.s, or why he's after Q.Q.s. But that doesn't matter. All you have to do is find everyone with either set of initials."

"Oh...oh, right..."

But on August 16th, they were speaking in hindsight, they were much too late, and the third murder had long since happened. Just to be sure, she had checked, and within five hundred meters of Glass Station there was no one with the initials Q.Q., and only one person with the initials B.B.—the third victim, Backyard Bottomslash.

The eyeglass message was very simple compared to the bookshelf message at the first scene, but they had only been able to solve it because they already had the phrase Glass Station in mind—otherwise, who would ever be able to figure out that putting glasses on a corpse was a message from the killer? The very simplicity of it was exactly what made it even more difficult than the first murder. Now Misora had to stop the fourth murder, but would she be able to figure out the message left at the scene of the third? She was more than a little worried.

Once again, it was Ryuzaki who had brought up the topic of the victim's crushed eyes, it was Ryuzaki who had suggested she look at the photo album carefully—without him, she would not have figured it out. Or at the least, it would have taken a lot more time.

At this point, it was noon, so they decided to get some food and figure out how to move next. Ryuzaki invited Misora to eat with him, but she declined. There was no telling what hideous sweet or poison he would foist on her, and she needed to speak to L. The mysteries they had uncovered had reached a level that demanded reporting. She moved well away from the apartment, looked around her carefully, leaned against a wall, and dialed.

"This is L."

"This is Misora."

She was getting used to the synthetic voice. She quickly explained what had happened that day, and what they had figured out, wasting no words. She felt herself getting a little worked up when she was explaining why the victim had been lying face down, but repressed it. At least, she thought she had.

"Okay. I understand. I was right to pick you, Naomi Misora. Honestly, I did not expect such impressive results."

"No...not at all. I don't deserve the compliment. More importantly, about what I should do next...any thoughts? We don't know when the fourth murder will occur, so I thought maybe I should head right over to West L.A. now..."

"No need," L said. "I'd prefer that you secure your footing. Based on your report, there is plenty of time before the fourth murder occurs."

"Eh?"

She hadn't said anything like that...had she?

"The killer will take his fourth victim on August 22nd. You have six more days."

"Six days?"

That was nine days after the third murder. Nine days, four days, nine days...and nine days again? What was he basing this assumption on? Misora was about to voice this question, but...

"I'm afraid I don't have time to explain right now," he said. "Please try and work it out for yourself. But the next murder will occur...or the killer will make his next attempt on the 22nd, and I would have you act on that assumption."

"Understood."

He didn't sound like he was in the mood for arguments. But August 22nd...come to think of it, the LAPD had received the crossword puzzle on July 22nd. The same day of the month. Was that a connection?

"In that case, over the next six days I will make careful preparations and investigate the third crime scene."

"Please do. Oh, and—Naomi Misora, do take all precautions for your own safety. You are the only person who can work for me on this case. If you fall, there is no one who can replace you."

He must be referring to the fight in the alley. She was caught off guard by this. No one who could replace her? For L it might be a very casual pronouncement, or just an outright lie, but Misora found it hard to believe it was even being applied to her.

"Don't worry. I wasn't hurt."

"No—I mean, take care not to place yourself in a situation in which you might be attacked. Avoid back roads, alleys, and other deserted areas. It might take longer, but stick to crowded areas and busy streets."

"I'm fine, L. And I can take care of myself. I've trained in martial arts."

"Have you? In what? Karate? Or judo?"

"Capoeira."

"…"

Even over the scrambled line, she could tell L wasn't sure how to respond. She admitted capoeira was an unusual choice for a Japanese FBI agent. Misora felt a moment's gleeful pride, as if she'd outsmarted L—though she knew she had done nothing of the kind.

"Yeah, I thought it was crap till I actually started it, but I got involved in street dancing in college and joined a capoeira group as an extension of that. It's actually a really effective form of self-defense for a woman. The basic techniques all involve dodging your opponent's attacks, which means it isn't possible to overpower a block like it is in karate or judo. We can never match a man for power. And the acrobatic, tricky movements in capoeira give you time to get a good look at your assailant."

"Really? That makes sense," L said, sounding impressed.

Genuinely impressed, not just saying so.

"Your description makes it sound interesting. If I have time, I will have to look at some videos…but however confident you are, if they have a gun, or outnumber you, the situation changes. Take all the precautions you can."

"Of course. Don't worry, I always do. Um, L…" Misora said at last.

"What is it, Naomi Misora?"

"I was wondering…you've figured out what the killer's goal is, right?"

"…Yes," he said, after a long pause.

Misora nodded. Otherwise, he wouldn't have been so sure when the fourth murder would occur. But he had told her to figure the reason out for herself. Which meant he had enough information to identify the killer now? Just as this thought crossed Misora's mind, L destroyed her chain of thought with a single phrase.

"To tell the truth, I always knew who the killer was."

"…Eh?"

"The killer…" L said, " is B."

We were raised at Wammy's House in England, in Winchester, as L's successors, as L's alternatives, but that does not mean we knew anything more about L than anybody else. Including myself, only a few of us ever met L as L, and even I know nothing about L before he met Watari—Quillish Wammy, the genius inventor who founded Wammy's House. Nobody knows what's going on in L's head. But even so, I know how Watari felt. Looking at L's incredible talents from the perspective of an inventor—of course he wanted to make a copy, of course he wanted to create a backup. Anyone would feel the same. As I have already explained, L never appeared in public. L knew that his own death would increase the crime rate all over the world by a few dozen percentage points. But what if they could copy him? What if they could make a backup?

That was us.

L's children, gathered from all corners of the world.

Children gathered together, never told each other's names.

But even for a genius like Watari, creating a fake L was easier said than done. Even for Near and I, who were said to be the closest to L...the more we tried to be like him, the closer we got, the farther away he was, like chasing a mirage. So I hardly need to tell you what it was like when Wammy's House was first founded, when he was still experimenting. The first child, A, was unable to handle the pressure of living up to L and took his own life, and the second child, Beyond Birthday, was brilliant and deviant.

B stood for Backup.

But B tried to surpass L, not become him...no, that might not be right. I have no way of knowing the inner workings of his mind. He...*their* generation was not like the fourth generation, with Near and I, all the children bound only to the one with the serial L. They were prototypes, never even given the L code, expected to fail. I prefer to refrain from idle speculation based on my own experiences, but, well, Beyond Birthday may have thought something like this: As long as there was L, B would never be L. As long as the original existed, the copy was always a copy.

The Los Angeles BB Murder Cases.

L.A.B.B.—L is After Beyond Birthday.

This reading is why I think this name is so much closer to the killer's intentions than the Wara Ningyo Murders, or the Los Angeles Serial Locked Room Killings. I wasn't talking about the names on a purely stylistic basis. Whether Beyond Birthday had put that much thought into it I have no idea, but if he had a specific reason for choosing to commit his murders in L.A., then that is probably why. I am sure he had a much more personal obsession with L as an individual than Near or I ever did. I can understand why someone would become a criminal in order to fight against a detective, which is why I can write about it like this, but even so. What did he hope to accomplish by killing unrelated people? Or perhaps B simply wanted to meet L. Then he could use the eyes of the shinigami he'd been born with and see L's real name, see when L would die. He would be able to find out who L was. Beyond Birthday had never told anyone that he had the eyes of a shinigami, and it would not surprise me at all if he believed himself to be some kind of shinigami.

So this all boiled down to a strangely shaped battle of detection between L and B. It was not exactly the same as the detective wars L had waged with Eraldo Coil and Danuve, but just as the greatest of detectives makes the greatest of criminals, a specialist in investigation is also a specialist in murder. From this perspective, this was nothing but a detective war.

Beyond Birthday challenged L.

And L accepted the challenge.

To put it bluntly, the Los Angeles BB Murder Cases were nothing but an internal struggle, a civil war within our home, sweet home— Wammy's House. Unfortunate for the victims that got mixed up in it, but even if Beyond Birthday had not killed them, all those victims were fated to die that day, at that time, for some other reason, so logically and morally, their deaths were unavoidable. So in the strictest sense of the word, the only one who really got mixed up in their war was Naomi Misora.

"Mmm…mm…mm-hmm-hmm-hmmm…mm, mm, mm…Zo zo zo zo…no, that's a horrible laugh…henh henh henh."

He was ready now.

He cracked his neck…

And Beyond Birthday began to move.

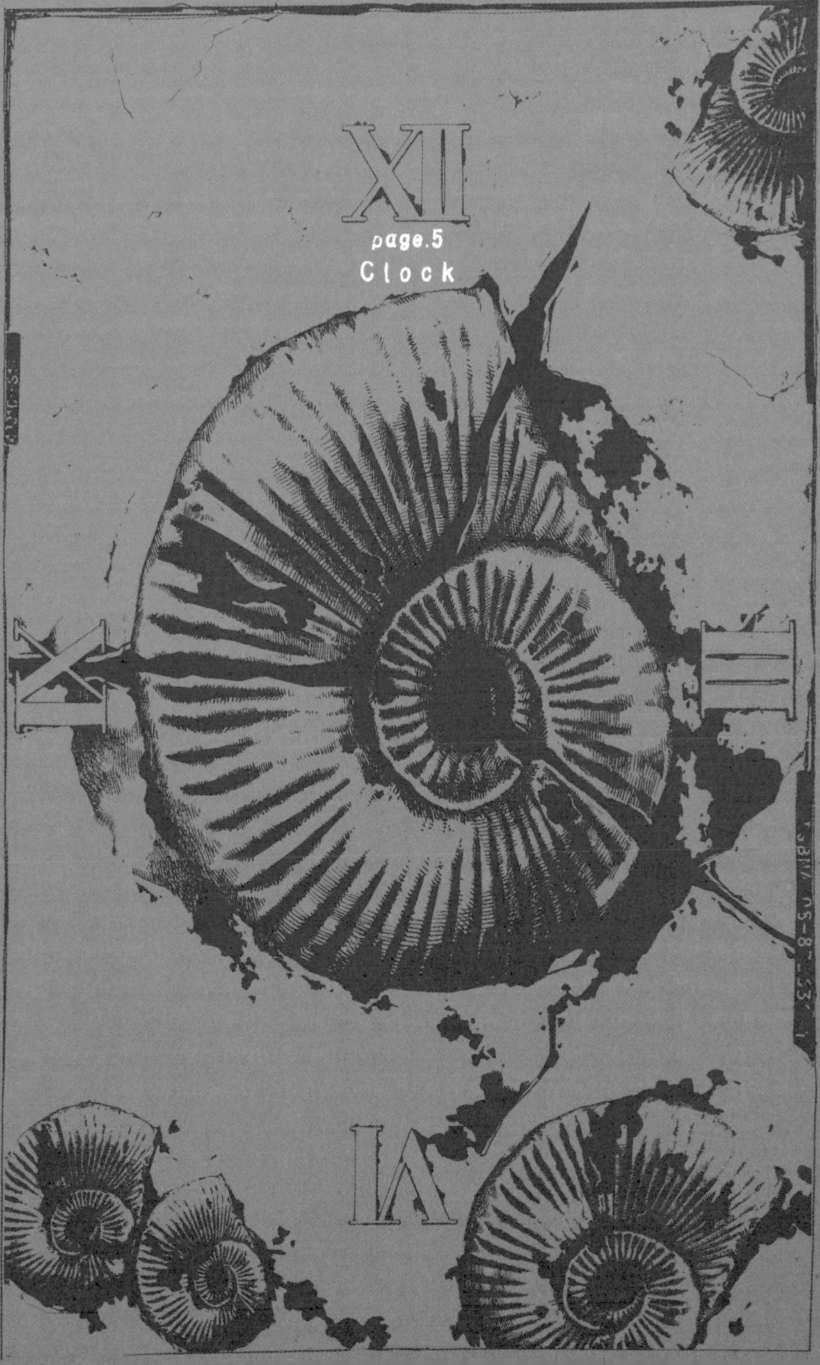
XII
page.5
Clock
IX
III
VI

Ryuzaki finally reached the townhouse where the third murder had occurred at just past three.

"Sorry to keep you waiting, Misora," he said, not appearing the least bit guilty about showing up an hour late.

"Don't worry, I wasn't waiting. I started without you," Misora said, as sarcastically as possible.

"I see," Ryuzaki said, going down on all fours and scuttling over toward her. She was getting used to it, but it happened so suddenly she almost jumped. She hadn't seen him for three days, after all.

On August 16th, after speaking with L, she had gone back to Quarter Queen's apartment and told him that the fourth murder would happen in six days, on August 22nd. Naturally, Ryuzaki had asked her how she knew, but Misora had no idea. And she couldn't just say that L had said so...but while she and Ryuzaki talked the matter over, Misora had figured it out. Her answer was more than convincing, but she didn't feel like explaining it to Ryuzaki, so she simply stuck to her guns. In retrospect, Ryuzaki had let the matter drop a little too easily...but they had eventually decided to investigate the third crime scene, Backyard Bottomslash's home, on the 19th. In the meantime, both Naomi Misora and Rue Ryuzaki would look into the background of the case and make other preparations for their investigation.

Misora had spent the time staying in regular contact with L, advancing her own theories and obtaining a range of useful information as a result (including some new discoveries the police had made and L had relayed on to her), but the truth was that, on the 19th, even after arriving at the third crime scene and spending several hours investigating it alone, she felt like she had made no significant advances since downtown on the 16th.

"Did you already check the bathroom, Misora?"

"Of course. You?"

"I glanced inside before I came upstairs. But that bathtub's ruined. Painted like that, the only person who would dream of climbing in is Elizabeth Báthory."

"He wipes every single fingerprint, but not a drop of blood. Finicky types are always like that. The killer honestly doesn't give a damn about anything but himself."

"Yes, I agree," Ryuzaki said, but despite his words he seemed to have no problems crawling around the blood-spattered floor...or did he just not care? Just like the killer...Misora watched his movements carefully.

"I don't think there's anything here," she said. "I went over it pretty carefully."

"My, my. I never thought I'd hear you be so pessimistic, Misora."

"I'm not...just, Ryuzaki, I feel like the focus of this scene must be the severed limbs. The left arm and the right leg cut off...this is the biggest difference from his previous victims."

"Like you mentioned before, something that should be here, but isn't? In that case, what we have to think about is why the killer dropped the right leg in the bathroom and only took away the left arm. A whole arm. Not nearly as easy as taking away two volumes of *Akazukin Chacha*."

"And they still haven't found the arm...it's not that easy to dispose of body parts, so if the killer took it with him, then there must be a good reason for it. I don't know if that's the message...or if it isn't a message, there might be some kind of mark on it that the killer doesn't want us to see."

"Possibly. That makes sense. But crushing the second victim's eyes pointed to our blind spot, and to glasses, so carrying away the left arm must mean something...but once again, it's the right leg that bothers me, Misora. The killer's treatment of it is so muddled. You yourself said that disposing of a body isn't easy, but neither is cutting one up. It must have taken ages. It doesn't strike you as rather dangerous to do something like that in a townhouse? There are houses on either side, sharing walls, and they might notice at any moment."

"Both limbs were cut off right at the root...the body was found over there. Right, pictures, pictures..." Misora flipped through the folder she had already taken out and produced the photographs of the third crime scene. The same picture that had helped them figure out the message at the second scene. She held the photograph up, lining it up with the room and pinpointing where the body had been. "It was over here, lying on its back, with the right arm and left leg flung out wide...hmm..."

"Well, if your theory is correct, we have plenty of time before the next murder takes place. Let us be thorough. Speaking of which, don't you think it's time you explained why the fourth murder will happen on the 22nd?"

"Yeah, I suppose."

Misora put the photographs away and turned toward Ryuzaki. He wasn't facing her. They'd known each other five days and had met three times, and it was becoming clear that Ryuzaki was not aware that it was customary to face the person you were speaking with. But by this point, she was hardly going to dwell on something so insignificant.

"It's such a simple matter it almost seems like a waste of breath. The third murder happened on August 13th, right?"

"Yes, you don't even need to check."

"There were Roman numerals on the first victim's body, but this time we have Arabic numerals. Thirteen...13. If you write a one and a three next to each other...they look like a B."

"Yes," Ryuzaki nodded.

This was so simple she had worried that he would laugh at her, but he seemed to be taking it surprisingly seriously.

"Come to think of it, I once saw a children's game show where they asked what one plus three equaled, and the answer was B..."

"Exactly. B."

"B.B.? But Misora, that works for the third murder, since it took place on August 13th, but what about the other dates? The crossword puzzle reached the LAPD on July 22nd, the first murder was on July 31st, the second on August 4th, and you've predicted the fourth on August 22nd...none of which form the letter B."

"Not at first glance. But apply the same principle following a different pattern. The easiest is the first murder...July 31st. Three and one. Reverse the two and you get thirteen."

"Okay, I'll grant you the 31st. That seems reasonable enough. But what about the fourth and the two 22nds?"

"Same thing. Just change the pattern. Take the problem you mentioned from the children's game show—one plus three. August 4th—four is the normal answer to that equation. And August 22nd... if you take one from the tens place and put it in the ones place you end up back at thirteen."

B.

Thirteen.

"In other words, every day the killer takes action, the 22nd, the 31st, the 4th, the 13th...the tens place and the ones place add up to four. In each month there are only those four dates that do that. Only four. And something happens on every one of those. Also, the Wara Ningyo started out at four. One plus three equals four. And this might just be a coincidence, but worth putting on the pile—the gaps between the cases, four days and nine days, if you add four and nine, you get thirteen…B."

"…I see. Not bad," Ryuzaki said, nodding.

Misora beamed.

"Picking up on the similarity between thirteen and B is a pretty good idea."

"Isn't it? So the fourth murder will happen nine days after the 13th, on the 22nd. Nine, four, nine…I considered the possibility of another four, and the murder happening on the 17th, but it seemed far more likely that it would be the 22nd. After all, something already happened on that day last month. And there's absolutely no way to get from seventeen to B, no matter how hard you try. So the fourth murder can only take place on the 22nd."

The 17th had already passed, and there had been no related murders in Los Angeles on that day. She had been a little worried, but the strength of L's declaration had kept her calm. She had told herself that four days and nine days adding up to thirteen had been pure chance, an irrelevant coincidence that the killer could afford to ignore.

"If I could add one thing," Ryuzaki said. "That particular method of transforming twenty-two to thirteen is a little forced. Bending the argument to suit your purpose—there's no reason to move the one from the tens place like that. It's not like switching the numbers from thirty-one to thirteen. That explanation was clearly created after the fact."

"Eh…but, Ryuzaki…"

"Don't misunderstand me—I fundamentally agree with your reasoning. Just not that particular point."

"But…then…"

If he refuted the most important date, the entire argument fell apart. He had effectively refused to agree with anything she'd said.

"But I have a suggestion. Misora, you were raised in Japan, right? Then you are more familiar with Japanese numerals than I am."

"...Numbers in kanji?"

"Visualize the kanji for twenty-two."

"??"

The kanji...

二十二?

She pictured the characters in her mind, but they failed to suggest anything.

"Well?"

"No, I don't know what you..."

"Oh...then let me try a hint. Misora, imagine that the middle kanji, the kanji for ten, is a plus sign. Which means 二十二 is actually 二 + 二...two plus two."

"Oh."

That wasn't a hint. It was the answer.

二 + 二 was...four.

And four was 一 + 三 was...thirteen.

"Add them together and you get four...and you already explained brilliantly that four was one plus three. After all, if one plus three is B, then we have to put one and three together, which is the same as one plus three, which create the shape of the letter B. That's exactly why we can read twenty-two as 二十二. We just need enough reason to add the numbers together. And with this condition, your reasoning for placing the fourth murder on the 22nd sounds accurate. I was somewhat bowled over by the force of your conviction earlier, and was a little nervous about following your lead, but now I feel as happy as if I'd drunk a mug of molasses."

"..."

That metaphor gave Misora heartburn.

But apparently Ryuzaki believed this was why she had said the fourth murder would take place on the 22nd. Not full marks, since his reasoning for the actual date was better than hers, but she could relax a little.

"But Misora," Ryuzaki said. "One more thing."

"Yeah?"

This was the second one more thing.

It caught her off guard.

"Your theory is based on the assumption that when the killer chooses his victims, he requires that they have the initials B.B. But like we discussed, there is still a possibility that the killer is after Q.Q., not B.B."

"Oh, yeah..."

If the fourth victim turned out to be a child with the initials Q.Q., lying face down, then their theories would be thrown out the window.

"If it is Q rather than B, then your theory doesn't hold water. You would have created it from nothing, forcing it into existence based on faulty logic. Based on coincidence."

"Coincidence...that the number thirteen looks like a B? But it's so blatant...and Q just fits in there so neatly..."

"Yes. I agree. I don't believe any of it was coincidental. But your theory is based on hindsight. Created after the fact. I want to know why you chose to build your theories on B, not Q."

"Well..."

Because L had said so. Rather firmly. "The killer is B." She'd known in advance. But she couldn't tell Ryuzaki that. She had to keep L a secret from him. She couldn't let her guard down and let something slip, no matter how much they spoke.

"...I guess with three victims...there were two Bs to one Q, and B just seemed more likely. I thought about Q afterward, of course, but I couldn't find any patterns that related to it..." she said, trying to cover. But even as the words left her mouth, she knew they sounded unnatural.

And sure enough, Ryuzaki dismissed it, "That's so arbitrary. Nothing to support it at all."

Her good mood was gone now. She bit her lip—she *had* reached those conclusions working backward, trying to figure out a reason for what L had said. L's word supported it, so it was probably right, but that didn't change anything.

"The killer is B..."

"What?"

"No, I mean, he's so obsessed with the letter B. Maybe that very obsession is part of the message, and the killer's initials are B.B. as well."

"Or maybe they're Q.Q. Like you said, a lot of elements of the case do point to B, but it's also possible we simply haven't stumbled across the signs pointing to Q."

"Yeah...I suppose so..."

"That said, I do think B is more likely than Q as well. More than ninety-nine percent," Ryuzaki admitted.

Essentially retracting the last few minutes.

"There's a good chance the killer's initials are B. The victims are all B.B., and the killer is too...things are getting interesting."

"Interesting?"

"Yes. Anyway, be careful next time, Misora. If you agree with something, you must have sufficient reason to agree with it. If you disagree with something, you must have sufficient reason to disagree with it. However accurate, a deduction based on a fallacy means you have not defeated the killer."

"Defeated? Ryuzaki, is this really a matter of winning and losing?"

"Yes," Ryuzaki said. "It is."

Because this was war.

L was said to never move on a case unless there were more than ten victims or a million dollars at stake. The only exceptions to this were cases at difficulty level L (extremely fitting), or when L had personal reasons compelling him to get involved. The Los Angeles BB murders were both of these. I hardly need to point out the difficulty by this stage of the story, and L was essentially fighting his own dead copy. The current head of Wammy's House had told Quillish Wammy/Watari, who had told L about B's disappearance in May, and ever since L had been looking for him even as he solved his other cases. Wammy's House only knew him as B—they did not know his real name, Beyond Birthday, so this search was near impossible, but L at last picked up his trail when the murders started—which is why L knew who the killer was. He had not been looking for a killer so much as he was looking for a case. L had been waiting, expecting Beyond Birthday to do something to challenge him. L could move any policeman in the world, but in this case, he did not ask anyone for help except Naomi Misora...more than likely, for this reason. I don't think L really put that much stock in honor, but everyone is embarrassed by their own sins, and nobody wants those missteps to become public knowledge.

L was the goal of everyone in Wammy's House.

Every one of us wanted to surpass him.

To step over him.

To step on him.

M did, N did, and B did.

M as a challenger, N as a successor.

B as a criminal.

"Ryuzaki, did you find anything new?"

Now that they had finished debating the matter of dates, Misora took a breather, went down to the kitchen on the first floor, made two cups of coffee (with normal amounts of sugar, obviously) and carried them back up to Backyard Bottomslash's room on a tray. She was holding the serving tray in both hands, which made opening the door rather tricky. Since the handle was at waist height, she was able to reposition herself a little bit and hook the tray on her belt buckle. She found Ryuzaki lying in the middle of the room, flat on his back, with his arms and legs flung out to the side. Misora froze in the doorway.

"Find…something?" Misora repeated, for no reason at all.

He wasn't going to make a bridge and start crawling around with his back to the floor, was he? Like something out of a horror movie…Misora gulped nervously, but to her great relief, this was apparently too weird even for Ryuzaki. But what was he doing?

"Um, Ryuzaki?"

"I'm a corpse."

"Hunh?"

"I have become a corpse. I cannot answer. I am dead."

"…"

She understood this. The word *understand* has a connotation of acceptance, which she sincerely wished to avoid, but it seemed clear that Ryuzaki had adopted the same pose as the third victim. Obviously, his left arm and right leg remained attached to his body, but with that in mind he did match the pictures of Backyard Bottomslash's bitter end. From a practical standpoint, Misora could not see any point to his behavior, but she was not the kind to interfere with other people's methods of deduction. Instead, Misora tried to figure out if, on her way to the desk, she should step over Ryuzaki or go around. She did not want to step over him, but it irritated her to go around.

"…Um…mm?"

And then she noticed. At least, she noticed that she had noticed something. But what had she noticed? Something had caught her eye…no, before that, the moment she opened the door her attention had been overwhelmed by the spectacle of Ryuzaki playing dead, so how could it have? That wasn't it. Then what would she have seen first if Ryuzaki were not lying there? If Ryuzaki had not been in the way of her carrying the coffee…if he had not been there…then nothing. The room would have been perfectly ordinary, if a little frilly. She could barely smell the blood. The only thing out of place was the hole in the wall…the hole?

"The mark left by the Wara Ningyo?"

It was just a hole, and hard to make out. But if it was not a hole, but the Wara Ningyo? Then the first thing that would catch her eye upon opening the door, just based on line of sight, was not Ryuzaki playing dead, but the Wara Ningyo. The moment she opened the door, she would see the Wara Ningyo…one of the dolls had been carefully placed in exactly that spot. And all the Wara Ningyo had been nailed to the walls at exactly the same height (at about waist height, if you were as tall as Misora) but the distance from the walls on either side changed depending on location. But at each location, when she had opened the door…

A hole.

"Excuse me, Ryuzaki!"

Still holding the coffee tray, Misora stepped…no, vaulted over Ryuzaki. At least, she meant to, but she was so distracted she missed her landing, and stomped on his stomach. In boots. And she reflectively tried to keep her balance, and avoid dropping the tray, which left her putting her entire weight on Ryuzaki's abdomen.

"Gah!" said the corpse.

Naturally.

"S-sorry!"

If she had spilled the coffee on him as well, Naomi Misora's reputation as a klutz would have been cemented forever, but in actual fact, the matter did not go that far. Her martial arts experience had honed her sense of balance. She put the tray down on the desk and picked up the police file. She checked to see if she had remembered correctly.

"What is it, Misora?"

Ryuzaki may have been an impossibly weird freak of a man, but even he did not go so far as to rejoice at the pain of a woman stepping on him. He stopped pretending to be a corpse, rolled over, and crawled toward her.

"I'm looking over the charts of the crime scenes. In each of them…I noticed the same thing. About the locations of the Wara Ningyo."

"The locations? What do you mean?"

"When we investigated the scenes, the police had already taken the dolls away, so I never noticed before…but there is a noticeable trend in the placement of the dolls. This scene included—when you open the door to enter the room, the first thing you see is a doll. There is a doll directly opposite the door—the killer arranged it so that when you come into the room, the first thing that catches your eye is a Wara Ningyo."

"Oh yeah…" Ryuzaki said, nodding. "That's certainly true for this room, and now that you mention it, I remember seeing the hole in the wall when I went into the first and second rooms as well. But Misora, what does that mean?"

"Er…um…"

What *did* it mean? She felt like it was a major discovery, and had stomped on Ryuzaki's belly in her enthusiasm, but now that he asked she didn't have an answer. Awkward. She couldn't admit the truth, so she scrambled to string something together.

"Well…it might have something to do with the locked rooms?"

"How so?"

"At all three scenes, the person who discovered the body opened the door and came in. Using a spare key or breaking the door down. They all came into the room…and saw that creepy doll on the wall. The Wara Ningyo was the first thing they saw. No matter what, their attention was drawn to it. Maybe while their attention was distracted, the killer, who'd been hiding in the room, slipped quietly out the door..."

"As classic a locked room detective novel trick as the needle and thread. But Misora, think about it. If you wanted to focus someone's attention, you wouldn't need the doll."

"Why not?"

"If there was no doll, then the first thing they would see is a *dead body*. Just like you froze when you came into the room and saw my corpse. All he had to do was slip out of the room when someone came in and was staring in shock at the body."

"Ah...right. Of course. So...did he want the person who found the body to see something *besides* the body first? I can't think of any reason why, but..."

"Neither can I."

"If he didn't want them to notice the body at all, I would understand, but what could he gain from arranging it so they didn't notice the body for a second or two? But in that case, why put a Wara Ningyo there? Is the placement just a coincidence?"

"No, I'm sure it was deliberate. It makes no sense to dismiss it as coincidental. But approaching it from this perspective doesn't strike me as very effective. Like I said before, rather than focusing on the Wara Ningyo and the locked room, I would prefer...I think we should concentrate on figuring out the message the killer left behind."

"But, Ryuzaki...no, you're right." She almost argued but stopped herself. It certainly was worth pursuing, but she didn't have any follow-through at the moment. First they needed to identify the fourth victim, or at least the location. There were Wara Ningyo at all the scenes, but the message was only in this room, and they needed to find it as soon as possible. "Sorry. I was wasting valuable time."

"I would rather you apologize for stepping on me, Misora."

"Oh, right, of course."

"You mean it? Then as a token of your contrition, would you do something for me?"

"...Okay..."

Could he be more blatant?

But she *had* stepped on him.

Very hard, with her full body weight.

"What?"

"Would you pretend to be dead, Misora? Like I was a moment ago. The victim, Backyard Bottomslash, was a woman, so you might provide more inspiration than I did."

"..."

Apparently this private detective was unaware that most people possess something called self-respect. But this was not the time to point this out to him. If she did, Naomi Misora felt she would be well on her way to earning a reputation as a *tsundere*—prickly to hide her inner drippiness. And the matter *was* urgent—she was willing to try anything that might help. She wasn't sure if this was one of those things, but by this point she was even willing to try crawling. Feeling oddly resigned, she lay down on the floor. The room looked really different from down there.

"...So? Anything?"

"No, not at all."

"Oh. Yeah, I thought not."

"..."

Futile.

Ryuzaki sat on the chair with his knees against his chest, pointed out that the coffee Misora had made was getting cold, and drank his. Misora had put sugar in the way she liked it, and half-expected him to complain, but he didn't say anything. Apparently he was capable of consuming non-sweet things too. It seemed she could get up now, but it felt more awkward to do so than to stay down here, so she didn't move.

"Whew...hot coffee helps the pain in my belly," Ryuzaki said.

He seemed so nonchalant, but he just wouldn't let that go.

"Ryuzaki…was this the same as the first victim? After she died, he took the clothes off, then cut off the arm and leg, and then put the clothes back on?"

"Yes. What of it?"

"No, I know it's easier to cut up a body without the clothes getting in the way. Clothes are pretty sturdy, really. They get tangled up on the blade. But once he has the clothes off, why does he put them back on? Why not leave his victims naked?"

"Hmm…"

"With the first victim, putting the shirt back on hid the cuts on the chest, or at least hid that they were Roman numerals. But this time…it must have been a pain in the ass. Putting clothes on a corpse…on anyone who can't move themselves…"

"…Misora, the leg he abandoned in the bathroom was wearing a sock and a shoe."

"Yeah, I saw the picture."

"Then, I mean, perhaps the killer's goal…no, the killer's message has nothing to do with the clothes or shoes, but only to do with the severed limbs. Which is *why* he put *everything else* back the way it used to be."

Put everything back.

But then…

"But then…the left arm and the right leg. He left the leg in the bathroom and took the arm with him…why? What was different about the left arm and the right leg? An arm and a leg…" Misora muttered, staring up at the ceiling.

Ryuzaki looked up at the ceiling as well, and said slowly, biting his thumbnail, "Once…on a different case…something happened that might help here. If you'd care to hear it?"

"Go ahead."

"It was a murder case, and the victim had been stabbed through the chest. Afterward, the ring finger of his left hand had been cut off and carried away. After his death. Can you guess why?"

"The ring finger of the left hand? That's easy. The victim was married, right? The killer must have cut it off to steal the wedding ring. Wedding rings have often been worn so long they can no longer be taken off."

"Yes. The killer was after money. Afterward, we successfully tracked down the ring on the black market and were able to trace it back to the killer and arrest him."

"But...that's certainly an interesting story and everything, but Ryuzaki, no one would cut off an entire arm to steal a ring. And Backyard Bottomslash wasn't married. According to the file, she wasn't even seeing anyone."

"But there are more rings than wedding rings."

"But you still wouldn't take the entire arm."

"Yes, you're right. That's why I only said it might help. If it didn't, then I apologize."

"Not worth apologizing for, but there was no ring...no ring..."

...So something *besides* a ring?

For example...a bracelet.

Not around the finger, but around the wrist...no, that was retarded. It made a certain amount of sense that you would need to cut off a finger to get a ring, but no matter how generously you looked at it, there was no reason to cut off an arm for a bracelet. Nobody would do that. And this killer wasn't after money, anyway. If he was, the second victim didn't fit.

"..."

Misora slowly reached her left arm out toward the ceiling. Holding it away from the floor. She opened her hand and stretched her fingers out all the way, as if trying to grab the fluorescent light overhead.

There was a ring on her finger. An engagement ring from Raye

Penber. An engagement ring that still seemed about as real as a joke between two children to her, but was it possible someone would cut off her finger, her arm, to steal it? What if it was a bracelet? No. Using herself as an example just made it seem all the more unlikely.

Holding her arm up like this had allowed her sleeve to slide down toward her shoulder. Her wristwatch came into view. It was a silver watch. A present on her birthday this year, February 14th, again from Raye Penber. So if it wasn't a bracelet, but a watch? It was silver, so it wasn't cheap...a watch?

"...Ryuzaki. Was Backyard Bottomslash right or left handed?"

"According to your file, right handed. What of it?"

"So...chances are she would have worn a watch on her left arm. So perhaps what the killer took away...was a watch," Misora said, from her position on her back on the floor. "The right leg still had a sock and shoe. So the arm he took away more than likely still had a watch on it."

"He cut off the arm to steal the watch? But why? Misora...you yourself said that it didn't make any sense to cut off an arm to steal a ring. So why would someone do that to steal a watch? If he were after the watch, he would have just taken it. Watches aren't like rings. They never get stuck. There's no reason to cut off the arm."

"No, I don't think he was after the watch either. But maybe the watch is this scene's message. If only the watch was missing it would be too obvious, so he took the arm too..."

"As a form of misdirection? I see...but in that case, we still don't know why he cut off the right leg as well. I doubt she wore a watch around her ankle. And even as a case of misdirection, there's still no need to take the whole arm—the wrist would have been plenty."

"..."

Yeah, true enough, but still...the watch idea itself still seemed like a good one. She felt like she was nearing the truth. If that same unnatural fixation, to use a cliché phrase, that she'd encountered at the first and second scenes was working here, than she felt like it would manifest itself this way...

"Left arm...right leg...left wrist...right ankle...left hand...right foot...watch...clock...timepiece...ticker...both hands and feet, both arms and legs...or are the bits left behind what really matter? Not the left arm and right leg, but the right arm and left legs? The four limbs..."

"Plus the head is five."

"Five...five minus two is three...three. The third scene. Limbs... and the head make five...the head? The neck...the neck, and one leg, and one arm..."

Misora was stringing words together as they came to her—but she was just spinning in circles, like a lost child, afraid of running into a dead end. The more she babbled, the more she lost the feeling that she was on to something. The hands of her compass were spinning...

"If five minus two is three, then he could have cut off both arms or both legs, or the left arm and the head...if the left arm had to be one of them, then why the right leg?"

Purely to fill the silence, Misora forced out a question that had not occurred to her, a question she did not even consider worth asking, but Ryuzaki took her up on it.

"The head and arm and leg left behind are all of different lengths..."

For a moment, she didn't know what he meant. It seemed like a total non sequitur, and her mind couldn't keep up with it. But an arm was longer than a head, and a leg was longer than an arm, but so what? Was Ryuzaki just blurting out whatever crossed his mind the way she was? But that wasn't going to help guide her compass needle...

"Needle? Or hands..."

"What about needles?"

"No, hands..."

The classic locked room trick with the needle and thread. But that had nothing to do with this...but hands? Could that be...

"A clock! Clock hands, Ryuzaki!"

"Huh? Clock hands...?"

"The hour hand, minute hand, and second hand! Three of them! Each of different lengths!"

Misora slapped the floor hard with her upraised arm and used the impact to push herself up to a sitting position. She moved quickly over to Ryuzaki, grabbed the coffee cup from him, drank the contents in a single gulp, and slammed the empty cup down on the table as if trying to break it.

"At the first scene he took *Akazukin Chacha* away to point us to *Insufficient Relaxation*, at the second scene he took the contacts to point us toward the glasses, and here at the third scene, he took away the wrist watch...and turned the victim into a clock!"

"The victim...into a clock?" Ryuzaki's deep-set eyes stared at her with a calmness in stark contrast to her own excitement. "By clock you mean..."

"The head is the hour hand, the arm is the minute hand, and the leg is the second hand! That's why the killer took the watch with him, and that's why he didn't just take the watch or just cut off the hand, but cut the arm off at the root and *had* to cut one of the legs off as well—otherwise, there wouldn't be three hands left!"

All that came out in one breath, and at last Misora felt her feet on the ground again. She took a picture out of her pocket—the picture of Backyard Bottomslash's corpse. On her back, her arms and legs...no arm and leg spread out, the left arm and right leg missing—Backyard Bottomslash.

"Look at this, Ryuzaki. See? The head is the hour, the arm is the minute, the leg is the second, so this is 12:45 and twenty seconds."

"Mmm. When you put it that way..."

"When I put it that way? It's obviously the message he left behind! And he tossed the leg into the bathroom because it was only the watch he needed to take away, and he wanted to emphasize that!"

"…"

Ryuzaki fell silent, apparently thinking.

"Let me see that," he said, taking the picture from Misora's hand. As she watched him pore over it, turning his head at all sorts of strange angles, Misora began to feel like her theory was completely wrong after all. All of this was only useful if it led to a message, and if he said that it was a baseless coincidence it would all fall apart—her deduction had no proof, could never be proven. It had been produced by pure instinct. The battle decided by instinct—by her instinct she would be victorious, or fail.

"Misora."

"Yes? What?"

"Assuming your theory is correct…from this picture, there is no way to be sure that the victim's clock is pointing at 12:45 and twenty seconds."

"Eh?"

"I mean, look," Ryuzaki said, holding out the picture.

Upside down.

"Hold it like this, and it's 6:15 and fifty seconds. Or like this…"

He turned the picture sideways.

"Three o'clock and thirty-five seconds. And if you turn it 180 degrees again, 9:30 and five seconds."

"…Oh."

Of course. He was right. The picture was taken with the body vertically, so she had just assumed that the head…the hour hand was pointing directly upward, at twelve o'clock. But if you really looked at the victim as a clock, that was not necessarily the case. It might be, but it might not be. Just change the angle of the picture and there could be infinite possibilities. Or at least 360. The hands might not move, but the numbers could be placed anywhere around them.

There was no clue indicating how to place the numbers.

"If the victim represents the three hands, then this square room is presumably the numbers. The victim was lying in the center of the room, after all. And the victim was placed like this, parallel or perpendicular to the walls of the room, so I think we can assume it is one of the four patterns I mentioned. But four patterns is still too many. We need to at least get it down to two, or we can't really say we've solved the killer's message."

"The room...is the numbers?"

"Now that I think about it, the first message involved Roman numerals...which are often used on clock faces. But there are no Roman numerals in here. If only there were some hint to tell us which wall goes with which number..."

Which wall was which time...? But there was nothing out of the ordinary on any of the walls, nothing that might indicate a number. One wall had a door, and the opposite wall a window. Another had a walk-in closet...or was it directions? The compass again...

"Ryuzaki, do you know which way north is? If north is twelve..."

"I already thought of that, but there's no logical reason to assume that north is twelve. This isn't a map, after all. It might be east, or west, or south."

"Logic...logic...yeah, yeah, we need proof, or at least something reasonable...but how can we tell which wall? There's nothing..."

"Indeed. It feels like there's a wall blocking our path, too tall for us to climb over."

"A wall? Good metaphor. A wall...a wall..."

A wall? The Wara Ningyo were on the walls. There had been two of them in here. Did that connect? Did the dolls finally have meaning here? Misora half forced herself to decide she couldn't see anything else that might be a hint, and pushed her thoughts into that channel. The Wara Ningyo. Wara. Ningyo. Straw dolls. Dolls. Stuffed animals? Stuffed animals...in the frilly room. Too many dolls for a twenty-eight-year-old woman...

The stuffed animals piled against the walls.

"I got it, Ryuzaki," Misora said.

This time she was calm.

This time she did not get worked up.

"The number of stuffed animals...the stuffed animals on each wall. The number of animals is pointing to the time. See? There are twelve of them against the wall with the door. And nine over there...twelve o'clock and nine o'clock. If we view the whole room as a clock, then the door goes on top."

"No, wait a second, Misora..." Ryuzaki interrupted. "Twelve and nine are certainly true enough, but there are five dolls over here, and only two on the fourth wall. If we use four numbers to indicate a clock face, then they should be twelve, three, six, and nine. Not twelve, two, five, and nine. These numbers don't fit."

"Of course they do. If we count the Wara Ningyo."

Misora looked again at the two holes in the wall.

"If we add the Wara Ningyo to those two stuffed animals...we get three. And if we add the Wara Ningyo to those five stuffed animals...we get six. This makes it work. The third crime scene itself is a clock. The entire room is a clock."

Misora put the photograph of Backyard Bottomslash down on the floor, where she had been lying a moment before, and where Ryuzaki had been lying before that. Carefully, making sure it was the right angle.

"6:15 and fifty seconds."

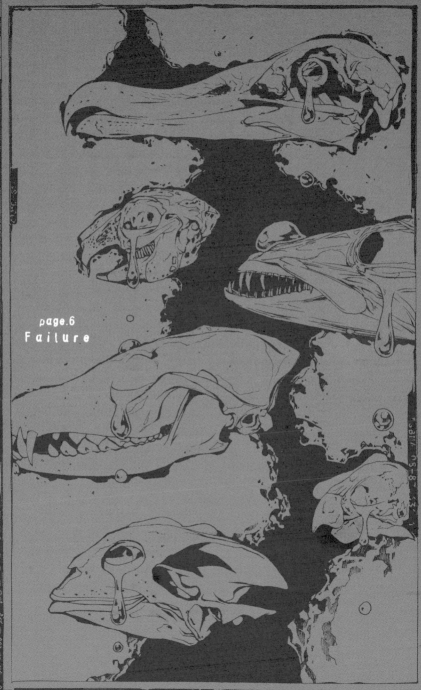

page.6
Failure

And at last, August 22nd.

The day the man behind the Los Angeles BB Murder Cases was to be arrested...but we can say that because we have history to tell us, and like all historical events, when it was happening in real time, none of those involved knew that, and the way events unfolded was hardly smooth sailing. In fact, Naomi Misora's day started with any number of inconsistencies and anxieties.

6:15 and fifty seconds.

They had managed to read that as the message left behind by the killer at the third crime scene, but was that 6:15 in the morning? Or in the evening? After they had solved the clock puzzle, Misora had searched the scene all night looking for anything that said "a.m." or "p.m." She found nothing.

"If we've looked this hard and found nothing, then maybe it doesn't really matter," Ryuzaki had suggested. "He made the victim look like an analog clock rather than a digital one, so trying to find something to indicate a.m. or p.m. might be a waste of time."

"Yeah..." Misora nodded.

Regardless of whether this was true or not, they had to assume it was. She began to decipher the message both as 6:15:50 and 18:15:50. The first scene had pointed them to Quarter Queen, and the second scene to Glass Station, so what was the third scene pointing toward? Misora and Ryuzaki both turned their energies toward this problem, but it was Ryuzaki who first came up with something. 061550. The construction approval number for a condominium. In Pasadena, in the valley, a massive complex. The sizes ranged from two bedroom to four bedroom, with over two hundred condos in all. And a woman named Blackberry Brown lived in condo number 1313. Her initials were B.B., and her condo number was too.

"It must be her," Misora said. All condo approval numbers began with zero, so there was no 181550. She had been worried about the a.m./p.m. thing, but now that they'd found the answer, she could relax. As Ryuzaki had said, with an analog clock it really didn't matter. Misora was greatly relieved, but Ryuzaki himself did not look very cheerful. Not that he ever did, but even so, he seemed particularly down.

"Something wrong, Ryuzaki? We've finally figured out what the killer's going to do, and can get ahead of him! We can lay a trap for him. Prevent the fourth murder, and if we're lucky, catch the killer as well. Nah—no luck about it. We will catch him, and catch him alive."

"Misora," Ryuzaki said. "The thing is, there was another candidate in the condo. Another B.B. A man named Blues-harp Babysplit, who lives alone in room 404."

"Oh..."

Two people with the target initials. In a massive complex of two hundred condos, not everyone lived alone—there were any number of people with families. Even if you downplayed that number there were easily four or five hundred people...and simple arithmetic suggested that one out of 676 people had the initials B.B. It was not particularly surprising that there were two of them in the complex. It was statistically reasonable.

"But," Misora said, "no matter how you look at it, room 1313 is our target. Thirteen is a code for B, Ryuzaki. And 1313 is B.B. The fourth murder...judging from the number of dolls, the final murder...what better location could the killer ask for?"

"I suppose..."

"I'm sure of it. I mean, 404?"

Certainly, four was one plus three, which was B, but faced with a choice between 1313 and 404 the killer would undoubtedly choose the former. No matter who the killer was, Misora was sure he would choose the former. But Ryuzaki apparently wasn't.

"Ryuzaki, do you know how rare it is for there to even be a thirteenth floor or a thirteenth room in America? They usually skip that number. I'm sure the killer would want to take advantage of that…in fact, he probably chose this building specifically because it did have a thirteenth floor."

"But remember, Misora. The number of days between the murders. The crossword puzzle reached the police station on July 22nd, the first murder happened nine days later on July 31st, the second murder four days later on August 4th, and the third murder nine days later on August 13th, and if the fourth murder is to happen on August 22nd, that will be nine days again. Nine days, four days, nine days, nine days. But why was it nine-four-nine-nine and not nine-four-nine-four? Even though nine plus four is thirteen."

"Well…"

It was Misora who had first pointed out that nine and four were thirteen. But since nothing had happened on August 17th, she had assumed it was just a coincidence. She hadn't been able to find a connection between seventeen and B, and it just hadn't seemed like that big of a problem. Misora had no idea why Ryuzaki was bringing it up now.

"We have a four. But three nines…it's so unbalanced."

"Yeah, but…alternating was…"

"Not alternating. Four and nine should be viewed as a set, and the numbers as a series of thirteens. But that hasn't happened…this doesn't strike you as odd?"

"…"

"But room number 404 gives us three fours and three nines."

"Oh…"

Was that what he meant?

"If it had been any room number other than 404, I would have agreed one hundred percent, no, two hundred percent that the fourth victim would be Blackberry Brown in room 1313, but since yet another B.B., Blues-harp Babysplit, lives in a room with two fours in the number…I can't ignore that."

"Yeah…I agree."

When he explained it like that, Misora was starting to think that room 404 was actually more likely. After all, she had been a little bothered by the gaps between the murders. Was it really okay to dismiss them as coincidence? Nothing had happened on the 17th, but that was after the fact. It had never really locked into place. But if the final murder were in room 404, it would take care of that a lot better than room 1313.

Misora clicked her tongue.

They hadn't been able to decide if the clock was a.m. or p.m., and now that they'd found a good candidate for the final murder scene, there were two potential victims…all this work, and the final piece refused to fall into place. It bothered her. She was sure they'd read the message correctly, but still doubts remained. There was every chance this would lead to some decisive mistake…

"Oh, well," Ryuzaki said. "We'll just have to split up. Fortunately, Misora, we have each other."

They might be working together, but nothing further.

But this was not the time to point that out.

"One of us should wait at each of the scenes. You take room 1313, Misora, and I'll take room 404. After all, Blackberry Brown is a woman, while Blues-harp Babysplit is a man. Seems like a natural arrangement."

"…And do what, exactly?"

"Just as you said, Misora. Lie in wait. Today or tomorrow, we should speak to Blackberry Brown and Blues-harp Babysplit, and get them to cooperate with our investigation. Obviously, we can't tell them they're being targeted by a serial killer. If they know too much the media might find out about what's happening and blow the whole thing."

"But they have a right to know?"

"And a right to live, which is more important. We will pay an appropriate fee, and borrow the room for the day."

"Pay?"

"Yes. The simplest means. Fortunately, my patrons are providing me with expense funds deep enough to cover the charges. If we solve the crime, they will be only too happy to pay. If this were an ordinary murder, this would never work, but these victims were only being targeted because of their initials, and there is no real reason for them to die. Their murders only have meaning if they are killed in their own room—whether that be 1313 or 404. So if we pretend to be them, and wait in their rooms, we should be able to meet the killer. Obviously, just in case, we should have Blackberry Brown and Blues-harp Babysplit stay in a safe place all day on the 22nd...put them up in a luxury suite at a four-star hotel, for example."

"And then we...I see."

Misora put her hand to her mouth, thinking. Buying the potential victims' cooperation sounded fine...she didn't know who the patron was backing Ryuzaki, but she should be able to get that kind of funding herself if she asked L. Ryuzaki would become Blues-harp Babysplit, and she would become Blackberry Brown...

"And we shouldn't call for police backup, right?"

"Yes. We might be able to protect the victim's life, but the scale of the operation would be too large. The killer would be more likely to escape. And our deductions are not enough evidence to make the police take action, anyway. Our reading of the killer's message is accurate at a ninety-nine percent chance, but however good it sounds, we have no proof. If they tell us it's all rootless speculation, we'd be done for."

"'Rootless.'"

"With nothing to support it."

"…"

She was pretty sure there was a different word for that.

But he had a point.

If she asked her boyfriend in the FBI, Raye Penber…no, she couldn't do that. Misora was suspended—and she'd told Ryuzaki she was a detective. Her actions of the past week could get her in hot water if the agency found out. Even if she was really working for L, she couldn't exactly admit that in public…

"The killer is presumably working alone, but, Ryuzaki, when it comes time to arrest him there will be a struggle."

"Don't worry. I can take him one on one. I may not look it, but I am quite strong. And you're trained in capoeira, right?"

"Yeah, but…"

"Misora, can you use a gun?"

"Eh? No, I ca…can, but I don't have one."

"Then I shall prepare one. You should be armed. So far this was merely a detective war with the killer, but from here on our lives are on the line. You should be ready for anything, Misora," Ryuzaki said, biting his thumbnail.

And so…

With any number of inconsistencies and anxieties, Naomi Misora spent the night in a hotel in West L.A. She called L from her hotel room and asked him for financial backing, and to check up on all the evidence they had uncovered. She wondered if L would suggest that lying in wait was too dangerous, and they should make the safety of the potential victims their first priority, wondered if he would oppose the strategy Ryuzaki had suggested, (part of her had hoped he would), but L seemed to be quite in favor of it. Misora asked him two or three times if she could really trust Ryuzaki, but he said again that there was no harm in letting him proceed. But of course, by the 22nd, everything would be resolved…

"Please, Naomi Misora," L said. "Whatever you do, please catch the killer."

Whatever you do.

Whatever.

"…Understood."

"Thank you. However, Misora, while it is true that we are unable to ask for help publicly from the police, I can supply some private backup. I plan to station a few individuals working directly for me in the area around the condominiums. They do not need any solid proof to activate. Of course, they will keep their distance, but…"

"Okay, sounds good."

When her conversation with L was finished it was past midnight—it was already August 21st. She would have to spend the entirety of the 22nd in Pasadena, which meant she had to arrive early on the evening of the 21st. With all that on her mind, she knew it would be a struggle, but she climbed into the hotel bed, hoping to get a good night's sleep.

"Wait…" she murmured.

As cobwebs formed over her mind, she murmured, "Now…when did I tell Ryuzaki about the capoeira?"

She didn't know.

And there was one other thing she didn't know.

Something she didn't even know she didn't know.

Something that she was never to know. No matter what she did, she had no way of knowing. That this killer, Beyond Birthday, could tell someone's name and time of death just by looking at their face, that he had been born with the eyes of the shinigami—she had no way of knowing that fake names were useless with him, completely and utterly pointless.

How could she have known?

Even Beyond Birthday himself could not explain how he had been born with the eyes of the shinigami, how he could use them with no payment, with no arrangement. Neither Misora nor L knew why, and, obviously, neither do I. The closest thing to an explanation I can offer is that there are shinigami stupid enough to drop their notebooks in our world, so there might well be shinigami stupid enough to drop their eyes. Either way, it was completely absurd to expect humans who had no idea shinigami even existed to be on the lookout for their eyes.

Even so, even with that in mind, she might have guessed. After all, B looks like thirteen, and thirteen is the number of the tarot card named Death...

And so.

With any number of inconsistencies and anxieties, and one significant failure...the story's climax arrives.

Case study.

I had originally intended to keep the reasons for Naomi Misora's leave of absence (which was effectively a suspension from duty) out of these notes—had planned to remain vague about all the details. If I could, I absolutely would stick to that plan. I mean it. Like I said before, she was the single greatest victim of the fallout from Wammy's House, and intruding on her private...or at least personal issues is something I am very reluctant to do. Which is why I have casually avoided any specific mention of it so far. However, since I now find myself attempting to describe the look in Naomi Misora's eyes as she grasped the gun Ryuzaki had given her in both hands (it was a Strayer-Voigt Infinity model), I can no longer skirt the issue. I can't just fast forward to the next scene without explaining the reasons behind that look.

That said, it's not a terribly complicated story. Putting it as simply as possible, the team she worked with had spent months secretly investigating and infiltrating a drug cartel, and she had blown the whole operation—because at a critical juncture, she had been unable to pull the trigger. While she did not customarily carry a gun with her, it was different on duty—nor did she have any intention of making pathetic excuses about not being able to shoot another human being. Naomi Misora was a trained FBI agent. She did not imagine her hands were clean, or that she was above such things. But she had not been able to pull the trigger. Her gun had been aimed at a child of only thirteen years...which didn't in any way excuse it. Thirteen or not, he was a dangerous criminal. But Naomi Misora had let him get away, and the secret investigation that many of her fellow agents had poured countless hours and an unbelievable amount of work into ended with nothing to show for it. Everything was finished. They had arrested no one, and while no one had died, there had been some agents injured so severely they might never be able to return to active duty—horrific results, considering the efforts squandered. Despite her own weak position within the organization, the fact that she had only been forced to take a leave of absence was rather lenient.

Naomi Misora honestly did not know why she had been unable to pull the trigger. Perhaps she did not possess the proper self-awareness...the proper resolve that an FBI agent should have. Her boyfriend, Raye Penber, had said, "I guess you couldn't live up to your nickname, Misora Massacre," somewhere between sarcasm and trying to cheer her up, but since she didn't understand it herself, she hadn't protested.

But Naomi Misora remembered.

The moment she'd pointed the gun at him...

The eyes that child had turned toward her.

Like he was staring at something he couldn't believe, like the grim reaper had just appeared before him. Like it was absurd—he could kill other people, but he had never imagined that he might be killed himself. But he should have known, he should have been ready to die the moment he first took a life. As any criminal would. As any FBI agent would. That threat hung over them all. She was part of the system. That child was part of the system too. Perhaps that had weakened their resolve. Perhaps that had numbed them to the threat. Perhaps their fears had rusted over. But so what? Given that child's upbringing, he not only had no chance to reform, he never had a prayer of living right to begin with. What had Misora expected from someone like that? How cruel was it of her to have expected anything? She knew as well as anyone that that child was living the only way he could. He had always been doomed. But did that mean he had to accept his fate? Was there only one way to live, one way to die? Was human life…was human death all controlled by some unseen hand?

Obviously, she harbored some resentment toward those who had used this failure as an excuse to expel her, but when she thought about the difference between the thirteen-year-old she had failed to shoot and the second victim in the Los Angeles BB murders, Quarter Queen, she began to feel like the whole affair was ridiculous.

Misora did not have a strong sense of justice.

She did not believe herself to be ethically or morally superior.

She did not approach work with any kind of philosophy.

She was where she was because her entire life had been like walking through a town she didn't know—if she lived her life over again, she was sure she'd end up somewhere completely different. If someone asked her why she was working for the FBI, she would never have been able to answer.

She was good at it, but that came from her abilities.

Not her thoughts.

"…What if the killer is a child?" Misora murmured, despondently.

"Thirteen...only thirteen..."

And she put the gun down beside herself, making sure the safety was on. Next to it were a pair of handcuffs, also supplied by Ryuzaki, intended for the killer. She was in condominium 1313, where Blackberry Brown lived. A two-bedroom condo, and the only room with a thumb turn lock was the room opposite the entrance.

Nine floors below her, in condo 404, Ryuzaki was also watching for the killer to arrive, taking Blues-harp Babysplit's place. He had insisted he was strong, but he seemed so scrawny and hunched over that she found it hard to believe, and was more than a little worried. He had seemed utterly confident when they had met up before taking their places, but...she had her doubts.

At this stage of affairs, Misora had absolutely no idea which room the killer, the man L called B, would come to—here to room 1313, or to Ryuzaki in 404? She'd been pondering the matter every second she could spare, but had honestly been unable to reach anything like a conclusion. And she was still bugged by the a.m./p.m. thing from the third scene...but there was no point in worrying about that now. All that mattered was to convince herself that the killer was coming here, to room 1313, to kill Blackberry Brown, and then to act accordingly. She couldn't afford to waste time worrying about other people. Or she could put it another way—B would come after her...*in L's place.*

She looked at the clock on the wall.

The digital display showed nine a.m. exactly.

Nine hours worth of August 22nd had already passed. Only fifteen hours remained. She was not going to get any sleep today. She would have to remain awake for at least twenty-four hours. She wasn't even allowed to take a bathroom break. Ryuzaki had advised her not to stretch her patience thin...she needed to be able to react the moment someone entered the room. But now it was time to call L again. She took her phone out of her bag and dialed according to instructions. Making sure the door and curtains were closed.

"L."

"Misora. Nothing happening here. I spoke to Ryuzaki earlier, but nothing has happened on his end either. No signs of anything out of the ordinary. I'm starting to feel like we're in it for the long haul."

"I see. Don't let your guard down. As I said before, your backup is in position around the condominium, but if anything happens, they aren't close enough to respond immediately."

"I know."

"Additionally, a few minutes ago I dispatched two people to the condo itself. I wasn't sure if they could be there in time, but the weather was on our side. We were lucky."

"Eh? But...that means..."

To avoid tipping off the killer, they had not even put security cameras or bugs in the rooms, much less the building—and that applied to extra people as well. They couldn't risk being noticed.

"Don't worry. There is no chance the killer will notice. One of them is a professional infiltrator, and the other one is a professional trickster. I can't tell you more, since you are an FBI agent, but basically, a thief and a con-man. I had one posted near each room."

"A thief...and a con-man?"

What was he saying?

Was this some sort of joke?

"So, Naomi Misora..." L said, wrapping up.

But Misora hastily stammered, "Um, er, L..." but then she hesitated, not sure if she should ask this or not.

"You...know the killer, right?"

"Yes, as I said. He is B."

"I don't mean like that...I mean, he's someone you know personally?"

On the 16th, L had said he had known all along that the killer was B, and she had sort of known ever since, but two days before, L had said something that changed her guess to conviction. *Whatever you do, please catch the killer.* The century's greatest detective, L, would never say that about some ordinary indiscriminate serial killer. And the way his name was just one letter long…

"Yes," the synthetic voice agreed.

As if he didn't mind being asked at all.

"But Naomi Misora, please keep that in the strictest confidence. The backup I have stationed near the condo, and the thief and con-man inside it have not been told what case they are working on. They are better off not knowing. Since you asked, I don't mind telling you, but generally speaking it was also something you were better off not knowing."

"I know. Either way, whoever B is, he is a dangerous criminal who has claimed the lives of three people for no good reason. But there is one thing I wanted to ask."

"What?"

"You know the killer, but you have nothing to do with him?"

This was…

…to Naomi Misora, this was about the same as asking if you could pull the trigger on a child.

"I have nothing to do with him," L said. "To be completely accurate, I do not even know B. He is simply someone I am aware of. But none of this affects my judgment. Certainly, I was interested in this case, and began to investigate it because I knew who the killer was. But that did not alter the way I investigated it, or the manner in which my investigation proceeded. Naomi Misora, I cannot overlook evil. I cannot forgive it. It does not matter if I know the person who commits evil or not. I am only interested in justice."

"Only…in justice…" Misora gasped. "Then…nothing else matters?"

"I wouldn't say that, but it is not a priority."

"You won't forgive any evil, no matter what the evil is?"

"I wouldn't say that, but it is not a priority."

"But…"

Like a thirteen-year-old victim.

"There are people who justice cannot save."

Like a thirteen-year-old criminal.

"And there are people who evil can save."

"There are. But even so," L said, his tone not changing at all.

As if gently admonishing Naomi Misora.

"Justice has more power than anything else."

"Power? By power…you mean strength?"

"No. I mean kindness."

He said it so easily.

Misora almost dropped the phone.

L

The century's greatest detective, L.

The detective of justice, L.

Who solved every case, no matter how difficult…

"…I misunderstood you, L."

"Did you? Well, I'm glad we cleared that up."

"I'll go back to work now."

"Very well."

She folded her phone and closed her eyes.

Whew.

She did not find herself spinning.

She had just heard a word that sounded good to her.

She'd been told something she needed to hear.

Perhaps she'd just been manipulated.

None of her problems had been solved. Her confusion remained. She still lacked resolve. She felt like something had changed, but by tomorrow it would undoubtedly be back to normal. But even so, for the moment, she was not going to make a fast decision, she was not going to turn in her resignation. When her leave of absence ended, she would go back to the FBI. In that moment, Naomi Misora made up her mind. And the killer from this case might make a nice souvenir.

"...So, in one hour, I have to call Ryuzaki...hope he's okay."

Blackberry Brown and Blues-harp Babysplit. Two B.B.s. Room 1313 and room 404...had there really been nothing in the third scene that could have eliminated one of them from consideration? She couldn't shake the idea that there had been. They had not been able to trim the possibilities down all the way because they had not done everything they could, they had not done everything they should...

"Oh. I see. That's why Q.Q.?"

She had hit upon something. The reason why the second victim had been Q.Q., not B.B. The reason he had turned the child over, turning b into q. To prevent the possibility of there being someone else with the same name. The type of message left behind at the first scene...a message pointing not at the place, but at the victim targeted...that kind of message always left the possibility of someone else with that name. Which is why he had chosen Q.Q.—much less common than B.B. Quarter Queen. Misora had no idea how many other Believe Bridesmaids or Backyard Bottomslashes there were in Los Angeles, but she did know that the girl had been the only Quarter Queen. Which meant they were right, and the link had been the Bs, not the Qs.

B.B.

But even though the killer had worked so hard to make sure the message could only be one person, why had the final problem allowed for two candidates? She must be overlooking some critical piece of the puzzle. There must be something she should have done...

The crossword puzzle.

She had never tried it.

...Now that she thought about it, there were any number of

problems she had been putting off thinking about. Not only the problem of which room. If they caught the killer, then everything would be explained, or…

"…The locked rooms. Did he really just have a key?"

In that case, he must have gone about his murders after preparing the key in advance…he must have investigated his victims for some time before the murders took place. They had done everything they could to avoid detection, but it was more than possible he knew Misora was waiting here for him…

"A needle and thread locked room…and the needle ended up being a useful hint at the third scene. Even if it was just free association…"

Needle, hand, clock hand.

And she had been surprised to find that the Wara Ningyo had a practical meaning…the previous scenes had suggested they were nothing but a metaphor for the victims. But they had been counted with the stuffed animals, adding up to the numbers of the four clock sides. So perhaps some of those stuffed animals didn't belong to the victim…to make sure the numbers matched. Seemed likely.

Four, three, two…the number of Wara Ningyo was decreasing.

The last one would appear at the fourth murder scene.

If there was a fourth.

"The final Wara Ningyo…I assume it'll be placed directly opposite the door? Seems most likely…most significant…but what is the significance? The first thing you see when you step into the locked room…catches your eye before you see the body…"

Without any clear idea what she was thinking, Misora stood up and moved over to the door. Turning her back to the door, she looked around the room—it was just a room, nothing out of the ordinary. At the moment, it wasn't even a crime scene. Nothing here but the signs of Blackberry Brown's life.

"The Wara Ningyo were always nailed at about the same

height...the horizontal placement was all over the place, but the vertical was basically the same. About waist height on me...so about this high..."

Misora crouched down.

Naturally, this meant she was sitting in a position very like Ryuzaki's habitual knee hug, but she tried not to think about that. If he was right, and this did make deduction easier, then it was even a good thing. She was alone in the room anyway. Assuming the fourth scene would follow the rule, and the Wara Ningyo was to be placed opposite the door, then from this position her eyes would meet the doll's, their sightlines at exactly the same height. Of course, Wara Ningyo had no eyes, and this wasn't getting her anywhere.

"Just because they were mixed in with the stuffed animals, there was no need for it to be opposite the door...if the placement is significant...the placement...or is it just another manifestation of his finicky nature...ow!"

Thinking too hard in an awkward sitting position had caused her to lose her balance and thump the back of her head on the doorknob. Rubbing the pain away, Misora turned absently to look behind her...and...

Her eyes lit upon the doorknob, and.

And just below it, the thumb turn lock. The latch.

"!!"

Misora's head snapped around so fast it made an audible whooshing noise, and she looked at the opposite wall again. There was nothing there, just an unbroken stretch of wallpaper. But Misora had just been imagining a Wara Ningyo hanging there. But a Wara Ningyo nailed at that height was *not* opposite the door.

It was opposite the door*knob*.

The doll was directly across from the thumb turn lock.

"Oh...how did I not notice that?!"

Waist height—she had known that was where the Wara Ningyo

were placed since she first saw the police file. At the first crime scene, when she had turned the thumb turn lock she had consciously noticed that the grip was at her waist height, and at the second scene she had thought clearly that the design of the apartment door was different, but it was of the same construction...and at the third scene she had turned the knob and opened the door while balancing a serving tray on her belt buckle. And it was easy enough to figure out that the Wara Ningyo and the thumb turn locks were at the same height. She did not even need to open the file and compare measurements. But so what? So what if the Wara Ningyo were nailed to the wall at the same height as the thumb turn locks...and the Wara Ningyo were placed directly opposite the latch of said thumb turn lock? Was there some reason for that?

"..."

She was headed for an answer she should not have headed for.

She would reach an answer she should not reach.

At this rate...

...she knew she would.

An answer that would overturn, uproot everything she had believed about this case...and she couldn't stop herself. She was past the point of being consciously capable of interrupting her deductions. Assuming that there was to be a Wara Ningyo placed on the wall opposite the door at the fourth scene...proof by contradiction. Four dolls, three, two, one!

"No, that doesn't make sense...that can't possibly be true...the locked room trick? The needle and thread locked room...the needle was at the third scene...and the thread? Under the crack in the door...the crack...the space...no space, tightly packed..."

A locked room.

A locked room...was usually created to make it look like the victim had committed suicide. But in this case, there was nothing like that...which meant if you flipped the idea...then the locked rooms existed to make a suicide look like a murder.

What then?

What then?

"Ah…"

In truth…

All along, Naomi Misora had done nothing that Ryuzaki had not manipulated her into. There was no point now in going back as far as the similarity between q and b they had discovered in the bookshelf message, but her conclusions about the date of the murder had changed shape dramatically while she was talking to Ryuzaki, and the notion that the third murder looked like a clock…Ryuzaki had led her to that from the moment she noticed the watch was missing. He had brought up the wedding ring, he had pointed out that the head and arm and leg were different lengths, he had suggested the walls as sides of the clock…Naomi Misora had been controlled like a puppet on strings.

"Oh, right…how did he know?"

But now at last.

Naomi Misora figured something out on her own.

Truth.

And justice.

"Aaaaaaaaaaaaaaaaaaaaaaaaaaaaaaaaaaaaaaaaaaaaaaaaaaauuuuuuu uuuuuuuuuuuugggggggggghhhhhhhhhhhhhhhhhh!"

Completely forgetting all notions of how she presented herself, Misora let out a howl that cracked the air around her. She jumped to her feet, leapt across the room, and grabbing her gun and handcuffs off the table, she spun around, flipped open the thumb turn lock, and burst out of room 1313.

Elevator.

No, not enough time. Emergency stairs.

Racking her brain for details of the complex's floor plan, which she had poured over the day before, Misora headed for the emergency stairs, kicking open the door and hurtling down them three or four stairs at a time.

Down.

Nine floors down.

"Damn it...damn it, damn it, damn it, damn it, damn it! Why why why why why...how can this be?! It's so god damn obvious!"

It pissed her off.

Wasn't the truth supposed to set you free? When the truth revealed itself, weren't you supposed to feel better? But if *this* was how things really were, then...

The century's greatest detective, advertised as solving every case imaginable, how great must his burden be, how much pain must he go through at every single moment...past, present, and future.

A burden so great it would leave you hunched over.

A bitter taste in your mouth that would leave you longing for sweets.

She was going so fast she almost missed her floor and had to brake hard. She paused for just a second to catch her breath, then opened the door and checked once more to make sure she was on the fourth floor. Which way? Right? Left? The complex shifted halfway up, and the corridors ran in different directions than the thirteenth floor...417 was on her right, and 418 beyond it, so this way!

"Aiieeee!"

Someone screamed.

Misora stiffened, but it was a woman's scream. She turned to look, and a resident had apparently come out of her apartment and seen Misora holding a gun. Distracting! Misora stepped away from the resident, running down the hall.

Toward room 404.

"R-Ryuzaki!"

Right round the next corner and she was there.

The front door wasn't locked. She stepped inside. 1313 had been

DEATH NOTE ANOTHER NOTE

152

page.6 Failure

a two bedroom, but this condo had three. One extra room. Which room? She had no time to think. She had to start with the nearest one. The first room—wrong. No one inside. Second room—the door wouldn't open. A thumb turn lock!

"Ryuzaki! Ryuzaki, Ryuzaki!"

She knocked…no, knock isn't strong enough, she pounded as if trying to break the door down. But it was sturdy and would not budge.

There was no answer from inside.

Ryuzaki did not answer.

"Hah!"

She half turned and kicked the doorknob with her heel. It stood a better chance than her fists, but the door wasn't breaking that easily. She kicked it again, just in case, but with no more success.

Misora aimed the gun.

Infinity.

Seven in the cartridge plus one in the chamber, a .45.

She aimed right for the lock.

"I'm pulling the trigger!"

Once, twice…she shot the lock.

The thumb turn lock and the knob burst off. She threw her shoulder into the door, and the first thing that hit her eyes was the Wara Ningyo. Nailed to the wall, directly opposite the door.

And next…

She saw a man on fire, in the corner away from the door. Flailing his arms around, unable to stand the pain of the flames rolling across him.

Ryuzaki.

It was Rue Ryuzaki.

She saw his eyes through the flames.

"R-Ryuzaki!"

The heat was so intense she could barely look at it.

The fire was spreading to the room.

A blast of heat struck her skin.

She smelled gasoline.

Strangulation, blunt force trauma, stabbing…and the final victim was fire!

She glanced at the ceiling—there was a sprinkler, but it had obviously been tampered with. It wasn't functioning. The alarm had been disabled as well. Misora forced herself not to panic, forced herself to take action. She bolted back out of room 404 into the hall, back the way she came. She'd seen a fire extinguisher on her way here. Just over…there! She grabbed it and ran back. She didn't need to read the instructions.

She pointed the end of the hose at the ball of fire, at Ryuzaki's body, burning red, and squeezed the handle hard. White foam sprayed out, coating the room, far stronger than she'd expected. She almost lost her balance, almost fell over backward, but grit her teeth and held on, not letting the hose move off Ryuzaki.

How long did it take?

Ten seconds? About that.

But Misora felt like the day was going to end before he stopped burning.

The fire extinguisher was empty…the fire was out.

The white foam began to subside.

And in front of her, a black, charred body. No, that was an understatement, soft-pedaling it. A better description would be a red-black mass of flesh. It looked like the flames had burned it all the way through.

The smell of gasoline hung in the air, along with the smell of burning hair and skin. Misora covered her nose. She glanced toward the window, wondering if she should get some ventilation…no, she couldn't risk a backdraft. As if afraid that any sudden movements would cause his body to crumble, Misora stepped gingerly toward

Ryuzaki. He was curled up, on his back. She knelt down beside him.

"Ryuzaki," she said.

He didn't answer.

Was he dead?

"Ryuzaki!"

"Ah...unh..."

"...Ryuzaki."

He was alive.

He was still alive.

He was burned all over and needed serious medical treatment immediately, but this came as a relief. She heard a sound behind her and turned around. There was someone there—the woman who had screamed when she saw Misora with the gun. She must live here. She had heard the gunshots and the fire extinguisher, and timidly come to see what was happening.

"D-did something happen?" she said.

Misora thought that "What happened?" would have been a better question, but...

"FBI," she said.

FBI.

She identified herself like that.

"Call the police, the fire department, and an ambulance."

The woman looked surprised, but nodded and left the room. Misora wondered if, in fact, this woman was the thief or the conman that L had sent here, but she could worry about that later.

She turned back to Ryuzaki.

Turned back to the red and black charred body.

And slowly took his wrist, still very hot, and checked his pulse...a little uneven, and very weak. He might be done for, might not make it to the hospital, might not last until the ambulance arrived.

In which case.

She had something to tell him.

She had something to do.

"Rue Ryuzaki," she said, putting the handcuffs on his wrist. "I arrest you on suspicion of the murders of Believe Bridesmaid, Quarter Queen, and Backyard Bottomslash. You do not have the right to remain silent, you do not have the right to an attorney, and you do not have the right to a fair trial."

The Los Angeles BB serial killer, Rue Ryuzaki, Beyond Birthday... was in custody.

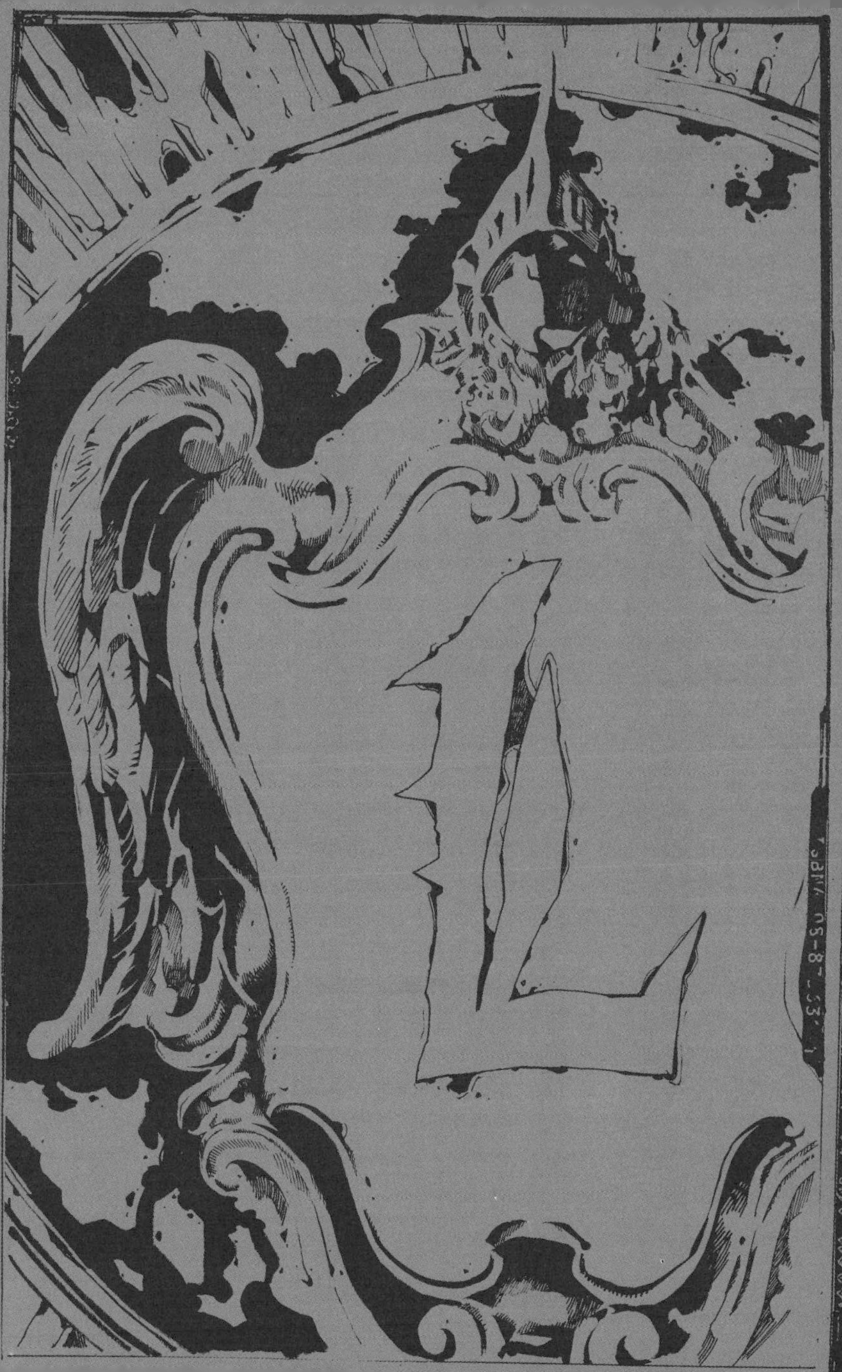
L

Nothing left but the explanation.

   There's not much left to write about here, so I'll settle for summarizing the key points. My great and respected predecessor, the man whose actions were a strong influence on me personally, B, B.B., Beyond Birthday—obviously, I need hardly explain again that the murders themselves were not his purpose. So what was he doing? Again, I hardly need to explain—he was challenging the man he copied, the century's greatest detective, L.

   A matter of winning or losing.

   A contest.

   But in this case, what would mean B's victory? How would he determine that L had lost? In an ordinary detective war, whoever solved the mystery first would win. Or if we look at the battle between L and the murderer Kira, L would win if he could prove who Kira was, while Kira would win when he killed L. But what about B and L? Beyond Birthday developed the following theory.

   Since L could solve every case no matter how challenging, if he created a case so difficult that L was unable to solve it, B would have defeated L.

   That was the Los Angeles BB Murder Cases.

   He knew that the moment he took action Wammy's House and Watari would alert L, so he did not even bother trying to stop them. He could only guess at which stage of his plan L would start to come after him, so he prepared things carefully, ready for L's entrance at any point. Beyond Birthday was careful, and finicky—and when L actually stepped in, on August 14th, just after the third murder, the timing was not ideal, but not bad either.

Of course, L would not move himself, but would carefully choose a pawn or two to work for him—at most three, probably two, and if B was lucky only one. Beyond Birthday was lucky. The eyes of the shinigami told him the pawn's name at once—Naomi Misora. An FBI agent on a leave of absence.

But what really mattered is that she was only working for L, and not L himself. Beyond Birthday was not battling Naomi Misora. He only cared about beating the one hiding behind her.

Which is why.

B approached Naomi Misora, calling himself Rue Ryuzaki.

Rue Ryuzaki—L.L.

For anyone from Wammy's House, there could be no higher goal than identifying yourself with that letter—and Beyond Birthday seized this case as his chance. Even Naomi Misora knew what had happened to detectives falsely identifying themselves as L, and B was from Wammy's House, so he knew better than anyone—so this choice suggests the strength of his decision. He never once intended to survive—he had made up his mind. He was ready.

And, as Ryuzaki, he had played the fool, observing Naomi Misora, occasionally guiding her skillfully, from the first scene to the third, making sure she gathered and deciphered all the clues and messages he had left behind. Compared to the challenge he had faced persuading the victims' family members to hire him to solve the case, leading Misora was undoubtedly a walk in the park. All the while testing her from this angle or that, seeing if she was worthy of serving as L's replacement...

Misora had contacted L on any number of occasions during her investigations. And she had clearly received instructions from L to allow this mysterious private detective, Rue Ryuzaki, free rein. He had expected this—he had sent the crossword puzzle to the LAPD

DEATH NOTE ANOTHER NOTE

160

last page

for just that reason. If someone appeared who had the sort of internal document that only someone like L could possibly obtain, even the century's greatest detective would be unable to dismiss him lightly—even though, in fact, Ryuzaki had the documents only because he had created them in the first place.

Misora had performed much better than he had expected. Like the moon has its dark side and every coin has two sides, Ryuzaki's hints had been blatant and yet unobtrusive, and any ordinary detective would never have been able to take them to their logical conclusion so effectively. She was everything he could have hoped for. The first three scenes all had clues that needed to be solved for his plan to proceed smoothly, but Ryuzaki could not be seen to solve too many of these on his own—just as L was using Misora to go after B, B was using Misora to go after L. Rue Ryuzaki could never be anything more than a suspicious private detective—not to be trusted, but not attracting too much attention from L either. As far as Beyond Birthday was concerned, the first three murders only served to set up the main act, the fourth murder. Misora had been the first to use the word camouflage, but in that sense, the first three murders were all camouflage, disguising the truth behind the fourth murder.

At the third scene, the clock had pointed to a large condo complex in Pasadena, in the Valley, where there were two B.B.s. This had not been hard for B to locate, with the eyes of the shinigami—that said, it had not exactly been simple to locate a place that matched the necessary conditions. Room 1313, Blackberry Brown. Room 404, Blues-harp Babysplit. Naomi Misora was working alone, which allowed him to avoid the need to use the backup plan he'd created in case L sent more than one person. If there had been two investigators, it would not simply have been a matter of finding a third B.B.

Misora in room 1313, and himself in room 404. Honestly, it did not particularly matter which room. Misora was in room 1313 for no better reason than that she was a woman.

And then Ryuzaki attempted suicide.

Turned the thumb lock by hand, nailed a Wara Ningyo into the wall, broke the sprinkler system, turned off the alarm, wiped the place for fingerprints, showered himself with gasoline, and lit himself on fire.

He had chosen himself to be the fourth victim. Beyond Birthday, the final B.B. That Rue Ryuzaki was a fake name did not even require L's resources—Misora was an FBI agent, and could find that out for herself quickly, and if she dug a little deeper would be able to find out that his real name was Beyond Birthday—B.B. More than acceptable as the fourth victim—and a highly appropriate end for the mysterious private detective.

Immolation. Burning to death.

Naturally, his face and fingerprints would burn as well—he had always disguised himself with heavy makeup while he was with Misora, and he had never left a picture behind, so even if someone directly affiliated with Wammy's House inspected the body, they would have no idea that Rue Ryuzaki/Beyond Birthday was B from Wammy's House. He had left nothing to connect Beyond Birthday to B. He had no intention of hiding his own identity (he wanted them to find out he was Beyond Birthday, to find out he was another B.B.), but he had to hide that he was B from Wammy's House. The reason he changed his methods of killing from strangulation at the first scene, to blunt force trauma at the second, to stabbing at the third was partly experimental, partly motivated by curiosity, but far, far more important was to make it seem only natural that the fourth murder was done with fire. And there was also the matter of the injuries done to each of the previous corpses—even Beyond Birthday was unable to damage his own body after death. It would never do to leave such an obvious discrepancy. With a burned body, it was impossible to tell if such damage had been done or not.

At the fourth scene, as I hardly need to explain, there was no message. There was no reason to leave one. B was presenting the Los Angeles BB Murder Cases to L as a case that could never be solved.

That L could not solve.

In other words, he had never prepared any clear solution to it—since the killer had committed suicide, disguised as the fourth victim, there was no longer a killer to catch, and no clues left to catch him with. Which is why the difficulty had escalated so dramatically from murder to murder. Particularly the message at the third scene, with its deliberate ambiguities—a.m. versus p.m., and room 1313 versus 404. So when no message was discovered at the fourth scene, Misora, and therefore L, would believe they had simply overlooked it. Something that should be there, but wasn't—and it was a lot harder to discover something that wasn't there than something that was. Especially if the missing thing had never been there in the first place—in that case, there was no way they would ever find it.

But how would they prove it?

A problem with no solution could only have one answer—that it could not be solved. But that answer conflicted with the fairness displayed in the first three murders. Which tied their hands. Unable to find something that wasn't there, L would have to continue searching for B—who no longer existed. The metaphor of the gradually decreasing Wara Ningyo established from the beginning that there would be only four victims, so the lack of further murders would not lead to the conclusion that the killer had passed away. L would be left chasing after the mirage of the deceased B. L would be forever followed by the mirage of the deceased B. L would spend the rest of his life trembling in fear of B's shadow.

L would lose.

B would win.

B was the top, and L was the bottom—L would grovel at B's feet.

The copy would surpass the original.

...Or so he thought.

In reality this did not happen, and the dizzying amount of time he had spent preparing for his crimes was all for nothing, destroyed, blown to smithereens—because he had focused all his energies on L, and never once viewed Naomi Misora as anything more than a pawn. All his attention was on the man behind her, and he never even saw Misora standing right in front of him. Even as he believed himself to be praising her skills, he ultimately underestimated her. She had done better than he expected—that very expression is, essentially, arrogant. If you ask me, even without Ryuzaki's hints, she might well have deciphered the messages at almost the same speed.

Naomi Misora.

The key had been the locked rooms. The locked rooms. Ryuzaki had said over and over that there was no need to think about them, that the killer had probably just used a spare key, because even he knew that focusing on that point could mean trouble. Beyond Birthday had a fair idea where the weaknesses in his own plot lay. But those were weaknesses that would be forgotten once the fourth murder happened, and if he could just hold out till then, if he could just distract her until then...then B would have won. That Misora figured it out just before the fourth murder was complete can only be described as a stroke of good luck.

At the first scene, and the second, and the third, the Wara Ningyo had been directly across from the door, and the dolls had been at the same height as the latch of the thumb turn lock—she had to notice both these things to figure it out. At the third murder scene the dolls had been counted along with the stuffed animals, which had seemed like a reasonable enough idea, but that was not their primary function. And their function as a metaphor for the victims was, again, not their true purpose.

Specifically, let us look at how the locked rooms were created. The doors were locked with a thread. The thread from a needle and thread. Misora had suggested running a thread under the door, looping it around the latch, and pulling on the thread to make the latch turn. Ryuzaki had denied it, but it had been a close call. She had been so close, but with that method, the force would have been pulling in the room direction, applying pressure to the door itself rather than the latch. As Ryuzaki had explained, the only effect would have been to pull outward on a door that opened inward.

But she had been very close.

At what she believed to be a potential fourth crime scene, Misora had crouched down in front of the door, putting her line of sight at waist height, and looked at the opposite wall—and imagined there was a Wara Ningyo there. Pinned to the wall across from her. Of course, the doll had to be physically pinned to the wall. There was no way it could just float there on its own—that would be magic, a scene out of a horror movie. It had to have been pinned there— which means there had also been some *thing* pinning it there. The holes in the wall at each crime scene—without even looking at the photos of the dolls in her files, Naomi Misora was Japanese, she knew about them as part of her culture.

Wara Ningyo had nails through them.

Long, thin nails.

And what mattered to the killer was not the doll itself...but the nail. The Wara Ningyo were nothing but a dramatic bit of misdirection. The shape of the nails...the nail's head. The thread went under the door, around the head of the nail, and from there over to the side wall, around another nail head, and finally back to the door itself, around the latch of the thumb turn lock—at the same height as the dolls. Obviously, this is a simplified description to make it easier to understand, and the operation was actually performed in reverse, starting at the lock, then going to the side wall, the opposite wall, and back under the door, but...essentially, the thread sketched a big triangle in the middle of the room. And if you pulled the string then…

The latch of the thumb turn lock would turn.

Click.

Essentially, he used the nail heads as pulleys, turning the power vectors diagonally. To be even more accurate, the Wara Ningyo was not placed directly opposite the door, or directly opposite the thumb turn latch, but directly opposite the gap under the door. This method prevented the dynamic force applied to the thread to be dispersed by the door. The thread did not touch the door, but simply passed under it, heading directly for the nail in the Wara Ningyo opposite—and all the force applied was transmitted in that direction. Then the nail head acted like a pulley, turning the direction of the force twice, and leading it to the thumb turn latch. Once the door was locked, obviously, he then had to recover the thread, so he had to use a particularly long one doubled over on itself…which explanation is just a bonus at this stage. As soon as he was sure the door was locked, he let go of one end of the thread and pulled on the other, successfully gathering all the thread to his side of the door. Anyone could pull this off, as long as they used strong thread that wouldn't break. If you have time, try it in your own room. As long as you are allowed to hammer nails into the walls.

Despite this tedious explanation, the exact nature of the locked room trick is completely unimportant. Well…perhaps not completely, but to focus too much on the trick itself is to miss the real point. What really matters is that to pull this trick off, you need *at least two dolls*—because you need two nail head pulleys. At least two. One on the opposite wall and one on the side wall. Four dolls, three dolls, two dolls—the trick worked at the first three scenes. But at the fourth scene, where there was only one Wara Ningyo, the trick could not be used. With only one pulley opposite the door, the latch would not turn. The thread would not make a triangle, and would simply go over and come back in a straight line.

So, as I have already mentioned, the final victim, Rue Ryuzaki, turned the thumb turn latch by hand. We only know that because the locked room trick was solved before the fourth murder took place—otherwise, the fact that the locked room had been created even with only one Wara Ningyo would simply have been dropped into the file with all the other data. The weakness in his plan would evaporate—as long as the locked room remained a mystery until the fourth murder, it would remain one forever.

Naomi Misora was just in time.

Ryuzaki himself had asked absently, "What for?" Why had the killer made a locked room that he did not need? That question. A game, for fun...a puzzle. Locked rooms were designed to make a murder look like a suicide...but in this case, the locked rooms existed to make the fourth death look like it *wasn't* a suicide.

To provide L with a mystery he could not solve.

Even if he could not solve it, it did not mean there was no answer.

Namely: it was unsolvable.

According to Ryuzaki's scenario, Misora would come running down the stairs when he failed to answer his phone as scheduled to find the Wara Ningyo on the far wall and Beyond Birthday burned to death—and if she had not yet figured out the locked room mystery, then everything would go as B planned, his plot executed perfectly. Since the locked room had been created even with only one Wara Ningyo, nobody would ever think of the triangulation technique.

If the police had not taken the dolls and the nails that held them in place away as evidence, Misora would probably have figured it out faster. But this was not a matter of luck, but all part of Beyond Birthday's plan. He knew all along the police would investigate the scene first. Beyond Birthday had coldly calculated that by the time L's pawn arrived at the scene, the actual Wara Ningyo and the actual nails would be long gone. The third scene was the only one where they might remain—and in that case, they were counted with the stuffed animals to make the numbers on the sides of the clock face, which would distract her. So the only thing that did not go according to Beyond Birthday's plan was Misora's investigative ability.

No, not ability.

Inspiration.

But figuring out the locked room trick, figuring out that the way the killer had locked the doors would only work at the first three scenes did not tip off Naomi Misora. Rather, she had begun to wonder how the killer planned to lock the door at the fourth scene. Or to wonder if the theory was completely misguided. Her suspicions did not immediately turn toward Ryuzaki. Of course not—she had been told no details about the connection between L and B, so it never occurred to her that Ryuzaki might have a reason to do something like that. She kept saying he was suspicious, but her suspicions had never reached any definite form. To theorize that the fourth murder would actually be a suicide required her to realize that the message had pointed to two possible murder scenes, that the two of them were lying in wait for the killer, and since one of those two people was her, the other one had to be the killer...but Naomi Misora was not proficient in the kind of mathematical deduction that was required to logically prove who the killer was.

But she had figured it out.

Because he had *known*.

He knew that Naomi Misora knew capoeira.

And in this case, the only people who knew that were L, who Misora herself had told, and the man who had assaulted her in the alley downtown—the killer. Misora had used a capoeira technique while fighting him. She had driven him off with her capoeira. Since the idea that Ryuzaki *was* L was comically absurd and completely unthinkable, then it stood to reason the man who insulted her was Ryuzaki...which led Misora to the truth.

Failure.

Beyond Birthday, Rue Ryuzaki's one and only failure. The only failure the killer who never made mistakes had made. If he had just rated Naomi Misora a little bit higher, he would never have let that slip. But it was too late. He might have been born with the unbelievable eyes of the shinigami, but he had no eyes for judging people… Probably a little too pat a conclusion to draw. A neat turn of phrase, to be sure, but that doesn't salvage it.

It is now an eternal mystery exactly how much of the truth L grasped and when. He might have known everything all along and put Misora into action based on that, and he might well have never figured anything out and been saved by her. Either way seems perfectly possible. But let us not think of such petty things. L is not someone we should speak of in such petty terms. As long as one thing is clear, nothing else matters.

B lost to Naomi Misora.

In other words, he lost to L.

Losing twice in one battle, unable to die the way he had planned, Beyond Birthday was taken to the police hospital, ending the serial killings that had begun a month before, on July 31st…no, July 22nd, when the warning first reached the police station. Apparently B had poured gasoline on himself at almost exactly the same moment Misora had arrived at the truth. It took a full minute before Misora burst into room 404. It would not have been at all surprising if he had died of smoke suffocation before she got there, or died before he reached the hospital, before the ambulance arrived. But he did not die. He did not die. His body was stronger than he believed, and his life went on longer than he thought. The hardest part of killing someone is to actually kill them—if he had been able to see his own life, I'm sure Beyond Birthday would have chosen a different method. My poor, poor predecessor. Not only was he utterly and completely defeated, but he survived, driving home his embarrassment…he must have longed for death.

Accept my condolences, B.

And with that, there is nothing more to be said in these notes about the Los Angeles BB Murder Cases. If I had space left over I had intended to carry right on into the other two stories I heard from L: the story of the detective war between the three greatest detectives, all solving that infamous bio-terror case, with guest appearances by the last of the alphabet, the first X to the first Z from Wammy's House; and the story of how the world's greatest inventor, Quillish Wammy, aka Watari, had first met L, then about eight years old—the case that gave birth to the century's greatest detective, the Winchester Mad Bombings that occurred just after the third World War. But however objectively I look at things, I do not have the space or the time. Oh well. In that case, to close off the file, I will wrap things up with a small description of something that happened to Naomi Misora a few days later.

With all that had happened, Misora's return to work was put off till September. Capturing Beyond Birthday had proved to be far better for her than she had ever expected, and nobody uttered a word about her acting independently during her leave of absence. While she was not popular at work, nobody denied that she was good at her job—at least, not outwardly. It was not hard to imagine that L had pulled a few strings on her behalf. From an even more practical standpoint, it was also not difficult to imagine who was the real source of the money deposited in Misora's bank account by a company she'd never heard of before.

On September 1st, she left her house on foot, headed for the nearest subway station. When she reached her office, her superior would return her badge, her gun, and her handcuffs. The thought was a little embarrassing, and she felt a few butterflies in her stomach, but when it was over she would be back to her old life.

She had spoken to L only once after the killer was arrested. He thanked her for helping to solve the case, and told her just a little about the background of the case. That B had been a candidate to succeed L, and that the pressure of that had driven him off track. At last she felt that she could understand Ryuzaki's previously incomprehensible actions, but she also felt like she only imagined that she could. It all boiled down to the entire case being a challenge for L, and he had killed people, and tried to kill himself, for that alone…but while murders could be dismissed as simple madness, committing suicide for such a stupid reason could not. Before he became like that, if only someone had stopped him…but that just shows how intent he was on his purpose. His own life was as meaningless as the lives of his victims, nothing but a tool in Beyond Birthday's quest to surpass L. It mattered more to him than his own life. Perhaps he was less intent than desperate. Nobody could have stopped him.

That was his resolve.

Which made him…so very strong.

Had he really been strong?

Misora wondered, remembering how he had nervously chewed his thumbnail.

Strength.

Strength Misora could never hope to imitate…

"Mmm?"

The station entrance had just come into view, and standing in front of it was an awkward, uncomfortable-looking man.

A young man, with an intense expression.

There were lines under his eyes so dark she wondered if they were actually done with makeup. Like he hadn't slept in days—no, like he had never slept in his life. Like his sense of justice would not allow him time to sleep, since he had so many difficult cases to think about, battling unfathomable pressure on a daily basis.

He wore a long-sleeved white shirt and blue jeans.

His bare feet were crammed directly into beaten sneakers.

"??"

She had a strange sense of déjà vu.

Like she'd seen him or met him once before.

There was something about him that reminded her of Rue Ryuzaki—of Beyond Birthday. But the resemblance was backward, like this was the original, and the other had been a copy.

"Um, have we...?" she asked, even though he was hardly blocking the entrance bodily, and she could have simply ignored him and walked on inside.

The young man instantly leapt at her.

Leapt at her? No, that's not right. He actually tried to throw his arms around her.

"Huh?! No!"

Misora instantly bent backward, brushing off the man's embrace, and moved smoothly on to the offensive. She lowered her upper body backward, spinning once in the air and raising her back legs like a scorpion, slamming both heels down onto the man's shoulders. Both blows hit hard, and the impact knocked him off balance. With a thunderous crash, he tumbled down the subway stairs.

Whoops. A little overboard.

Certainly, he had assaulted her, but Misora quickly righted herself and ran down after him. "Are you okay?" she asked.

He was lying on his stomach like a crushed frog.

"I see," he muttered, seemingly talking to himself. "Watching videos and seeing it for real is quite different, but now I think I understand."

"Hunh?"

What was he talking about? Had he hit his head on something? Her first day back at work, and already in trouble...

"Um...can you stand?" Misora said, reaching out toward him. The man looked up at her, his eyes in shadow, as if two holes were staring at her.

"Thank you," he said, and took her hand.

Misora pulled him upright.

"Are you injured? Does it hurt anywhere?"

"I'm fine, thank you," the man said, not letting go of her hand.

Even on his feet, he did not attempt to move away.

They appeared to be shaking hands. Like warriors on a battlefield, exchanging a firm handshake after surviving yet another bloody fight.

"You are very kind," he said, with something like a smile, and at last let go of her hand. Then he tottered away as if nothing at all had happened, slowly climbing the stairs again.

"Ah…w-wait! Just a second!"

Misora had almost let him go, but a moment later she ran after him, circling around in front of him again. She was an FBI agent and could not let an assault crime go unpunished. The young man was sucking his thumb. He did not appear to be at all nervous.

"If you aren't hurt, then you'll have to come with me. Sexual assault is a serious crime. You can't go around throwing your arms around women. What were you thinking?"

"…"

"Don't just stand there. Say something. This attitude won't make things easier for you. What's your name?"

Naomi Misora had asked his name.

The young man nodded.

And answered.

"Please call me Ryuzaki," he said, unperturbed.

Just like someone else had.

And a few years after his arrest, on January 21, 2004, serving a life sentence in a California prison, Beyond Birthday died of a mysterious heart attack.

Totally irrelevant to you who don't give a damn, but I am very bad at remembering people's names, and no matter how many times I hear them I can easily forget. When you reach my level, using a roundabout expression like "bad at remembering names" is far less accurate than declaring aggressively that you are good at forgetting them. Additionally, I am very good at losing track of things. The pen I was using just a moment before, the shoes I was wearing just a minute ago, even the book I was reading a second ago just vanish into thin air. But this is just a matter of losing track of them, not actually losing them, and I can always find them again soon enough (in other words, I am just as good at finding things as I am at losing track of them), but unlike things, people's names, once forgotten, are not soon remembered. They say that all memories remain inside the brain even after you have forgotten them, but I am sure that is an outright lie. At the least, forgotten names have been completely erased. What do I do when I've forgotten a name? Nothing much. Frankly, when talking with an actual person, there aren't that many opportunities to address someone by name. Unlike in fiction, it is perfectly normal to hold a conversation with someone whose name you do not know, which can be said for occupations and labels as well as names. Whoever this guy is I have absolutely no idea, but it seems like we have apparently met several times before and he obviously knows me—I have had any number of conversations like that, and they usually go pretty smoothly. "Oh, but maybe he only half-remembers me and is just making conversation without really being sure who I am," I wonder, and the conversation ends. That said, I once did this with someone I had honestly never met before, which depressed me. "He must have thought I was such a nice guy! So wrong! I'm really painfully shy! Antisocial!" But it was too late. Why am I talking about this? Because I don't need a Death Note, but I wouldn't mind having the eyes of the shinigami.

This book is a spin-off of the massively successful *Death Note* manga by Tsugumi Ohba and Takeshi Obata. I wondered what a spin-off novel would be like, and now I know. I am completely honored to have worked on something by people who have both dramatcally enriched my life. Personally I found this job to be extremely stimulating and very worthwhile. When I first started working on it the projected subtitle was *Mad About L*, but the tone of the piece was more serious than I had imagined. Instead, it became *Death Note: Another Note: The Los Angeles BB Murder Cases.*

I wish you all sun, sea, and books.

NISIOISIN